The Viking's Apprentice

Book 1 in The Viking Series

By Kevin McLeod

Kevin McLeod

#1 Bestselling Author of The Award-Winning Children's
Series, *The Viking's Apprentice*

The Vikings Apprentice

The Vikings Apprentice II: The Master's
Revenge

The Viking's Apprentice III: Journey to the
Other Side

The Viking's Apprentice IV: The Sword of
Vercelli

The Viking's Apprentice series is also in audio book
format. Please visit below to see how you can listen to these
books on Audible:

www.kevinmcleodauthor.com/audible

For Rachael and Elena who inspire me every day.

Acknowledgements

Thank you to Kathleen, without your support and encouragement this book would not have been possible.

Thank you to my brother, Paul, for his artistic skill and his unique brand of inspirational speeches.

Thank you to the editors who showed great patience and skill through every edit.

Thank you to every person who buys this book, I hope you enjoy reading it as much as I enjoyed writing it.

Prologue

Running now, faster and faster, following the glow of the safety sticks. Breathing getting harder, chest hurting, he keeps running, not looking back. Focused on getting out. Where are the others? He can't remember leaving them behind No time, no time, just run. He can't have seen what his eyes showed him, a trick of the light? Loss of air in the caves? Still, he runs; fear is driving him on.

Something is coming, closing in on him. He hears the footsteps, hears the terrible noise. Running faster, light now, can see the cave entrance, close now, so close. Grabbed from behind. Hands moving over him pulling him back, light disappearing, not close enough, now the noise is his, he screams, then nothing.

Chapter 1

Peter sat in his chair watching the clock tick slowly towards 3:30 pm and the end of the day. What made this day special was that it was the end of term, and the summer holidays were minutes away. Peter was in his last year of primary school and his teacher, Mrs Atkinson, was giving a good luck speech with a tear in her eye and a lump in her throat.

'I will miss you all. Yes, even you George.' Mrs Atkinson said, giving Peter's best friend, George Taylor, a knowing smile.

George turned to Peter pulling a face. Peter stifled a laugh and tried to concentrate on Mrs Atkinson.

'You're all going to high school where you will face challenges and have the chance to blossom into the fine young men and women, I know you can be.'

The school bell sounded, and the children cheered as they raced for the door, shouting their goodbyes to Mrs Atkinson. George blew a kiss in her direction and ran out laughing.

'Enjoy the holidays everyone, and enjoy high school,' said Mrs Atkinson, watching as another class of children set off on the journey to becoming adults.

Peter and George ran towards the school gates where their mothers were waiting. George pulled ahead, running through the gates doing a slow-motion celebration while taking the acclaim of the imaginary crowd. Peter, the school sports champion, didn't mind letting his friend win this race.

Peter loved the summer holidays as he always spent the first two weeks at his Granddad's house in Campbell's Cove. What made this year even more special was that George was coming with him. They spotted their mothers standing together in the crowd and headed towards them.

'How does it feel to have left primary school?' asked Peter's mum.

'Great. It feels even better to have the whole summer off.' Peter replied.

'What time will I drop George off tomorrow morning?' asked George's mum.

'Around 7, it's a long drive, and Granddad will meet us halfway.' Mrs Collins said giving Peter a hug.

'Ok, see you at 7 then, enjoy your night.'

Mrs Taylor and George headed towards their car. George gave Peter a military salute and laughed, shouting 'See you in the morning, Peter!'

Peter and his mum got into the car for the drive home.

'Has Granddad called?' Peter asked.

'Yes, don't worry he called earlier and everything's fine. He's looking forward to seeing you and George.'

'Great I can't wait to get there and go exploring, and show George the house and the caves,' Peter said excitedly.

'Please try not to run your Granddad off his feet and keep Jake under control.'

'Yes, mum. I promise everything will be okay.'

They arrived home, and as soon as they were through the front door Jake came bounding down the stairs and leapt at Peter. Jake, Peter's overly excited Jack Russell, was on his usual mission to lick someone's face before he would calm down. Peter bent down, and Jake took his chance to accomplish his mission, jumping on to Peter's knees licking wildly at his face.

'Get off me you mad dog!' exclaimed Peter laughing, while wrestling with Jake.

Happy that the face licking had gone well, Jake bounded after Peter's mum who was heading for the kitchen.

'Calm down Jake. There's a good boy.'

'Peter, go up and sort out your suitcase. I left your clothes out, so pick what you want and put the rest away.'

'Ok mum will do.'

Mrs Collins watched her son going up the stairs and couldn't help but think how much he resembled his father. Tall, with chocolate brown hair and light blue eyes, his face had summer freckles already. He was showing promise in athletics, and his room was beginning to fill up with medals. His intelligence was shining through in his schoolwork. She was a very proud mother.

Peter went into his room and looked at the clothes his mum had laid out. Mums really didn't know about fashion for boys his age Peter decided. He picked through the piles looking for his newest coolest clothes discarding the rest in a heap on the floor. That was where they usually lived after all.

With his case packed in record time, Peter took out his Nintendo DS and started to play MarioKarts, his favourite game. He heard Jake coming up the stairs and watched as he nosed open the door and jumped on the bed. Jake looked at Peter, wagging his tail, before spotting the clothes on the floor. With one leap he was off the bed and burying himself underneath. A perfect Jack Russell size bed. Peter watched and laughed before going back to his game.

Just over an hour later Peter heard the sound of his dad's car wheels crunch over the gravel driveway. The pile of clothes in his room began to move, and Jake's head popped out from under a jumper.

'Who is it, boy?' Peter asked, trying to wind up Jake, which was not difficult.

The front door opened, and Jake sprang into action, another chance to lick a face was near. Peter heard Jake crash down the stairs towards his dad and heard his dad greet the dog happily. Peter walked down and found his dad holding Jake, stroking the back of his head while avoiding a face licking.

'There's my big high school boy!' Mr Collins said.

'So how does it feel to be free of the little school?'

'It feels great dad, but I still have the whole summer to look forward to.'

'Ahhh of course. Now didn't Granddad phone to cancel this year?' Mr Collins said, looking at Peter's mum.

'Too late dad, mum already told me everything's fine.' Peter said

'Guilty as charged. I couldn't joke with him this year, not with George going too.' Mrs Collins said, looking at her husband as he continued his fight with Jake.

Peter's dad phoned for a takeaway as was traditional on the last day of school. When it arrived, they all sat down at the table to a lovely Chinese meal. They talked about summer holidays, and about Campbell's Cove.

Mrs Collins told stories of the famous caves, and of the sea monsters and dragons that it was said inhabited the area a thousand years before. All of this served to feed Peter's excitement about his holiday.

The only one of the family not interested in the stories was Jake. He spent the mealtime under the table on constant look out for dropped food.

After dinner, Peter went out into the garden to play fetch with Jake, who would fetch anything you threw. From tennis balls to sticks and even old shoes it didn't matter to Jake if you threw it, he would go get it. The bleep of Peter's mobile phone went off in his pocket, and he looked to see a message from George.

'Cnt w8 4 the Cove! C U 2morro.'

Peter replied to the text and headed back into the house. It was too dark to continue playing fetch, and he wanted to get to sleep as fast as he could so that morning would arrive, and his holiday could start.

Peter lay in bed later that night trying to sleep. He tossed and turned, adjusted his pillows, but he was just too excited to drop off. None of this was pleasing Jake who was curled up at Peter's feet and had found it much easier to sleep. Eventually though when Peter did drift off his dreams were full of Campbell's Cove and his Granddad's magnificent old house.

Far away from the bed where Peter slept, just outside Campbell's Cove, a shadow moved across a farmyard. Quickly and quietly, unseen and unheard, it moved toward the hen house. Nothing stirred; nothing seemed aware of the presence as it closed in on its target.

If you had witnessed this strange going on you would have sworn that you'd seen something appear at the hen house, then vanish through a wall. People would say you were mad, but those people would be wrong.

Hens began to squawk scared by the thing that crept among them. No harm came to them. It needs the hens. It needs what they produce. It has come for eggs. By the time the farmer had reached the hen house to investigate the noise the visitor had left. It had no interest in the farmer or his family. Not yet.

Chapter 2

Morning arrived, and for the first time since Christmas Peter was up and out of bed before his alarm. Too excited to sleep he busied himself getting showered and dressed. Jake did not seem to share this enthusiasm and remained fast asleep under the duvet at the bottom of the bed.

Mrs Collins was preparing breakfast in the kitchen. The smell of cooking drifting through the house finally persuaded Jake to get up. Peter was heading down the stairs when Jake shot past hot on the trail of bacon.

'Morning mum, where's dad?' Peter asked.

'Morning sweetheart your dad's out in the back garden. Goodness knows what he's doing out there so early.'

Peter wandered over to the back door, letting Jake out as he went, searching for his dad. Jake found him first, inside the garage, busy looking for something.

'Dad, breakfast is almost ready.' Peter said. His dad looked up and gave Peter a smile.

'I'll be right in, was just looking for something that your Granddad asked for. I'm not sure why he wants it, but he was insistent. Ah ha, here it is.'

Mr Collins took out an old, very large, suitcase from under one of the tables along the side of the garage. The suitcase had Granddad's address on it and was locked with a padlock.

'Make sure he gets this will you?'

'Sure dad, what's inside it?'

'I don't know, but your Granddad asked me to look it out. You can tell me what's in it when you find out.'

'It's a deal.' Said Peter as Jake barked and left the garage in pursuit of more tasty things in the kitchen.

After breakfast, they packed the car with Peter's case, supplies for Jake and the case for Granddad. A few minutes later George and his mother arrived. George was smaller than Peter with dirty blonde hair and blue eyes. He was freckle free and always wore jeans. No matter what the weather you would only see him out of his jeans when he was in his school uniform or pyjamas.

Mr Collins helped move bags from the Taylor's car. The parents talked while the boys played with Jake. They tormented the poor dog with a tennis ball the way young boys do. They were playing a game of Jack Russell in the middle that Jake just could not win.

'Time to go, boys.' Mrs Collins shouted.

'George, do you remember what we talked about?' Mrs Taylor asked giving her son a serious look.

'Yes mum, don't worry I'll behave.' George replied with the hint of a smile on his lips.

'Peter. Remember to keep Jake under control, and don't tire out your Granddad.' Peter's dad said.

'I promise dad, we'll have a great time and make sure Granddad's okay.'

After George was half hugged to death by his mother, they got into the car with Mrs Collins and set out on the journey to meet Granddad.

The boys spent the journey time playing Nintendo and bugging Mrs Collins to change the music to something they had heard of. Mrs Collins just smiled and kept her music on, safe in the knowledge that in a few years the boys would love Bob Dylan. Didn't everyone eventually? Jake spent the journey asleep in his dog crate.

They arrived in the small town of Laderidge where they would meet Granddad, and the boys and Jake would continue on their journey. Granddad was already there standing next to his car in the public car park. He was dressed, as always, in one of his many green tweed suits with a slightly faded brown hat.

He saw them and waved, pointing for Mrs Collins to park next to him. Granddad was tall with silvery white hair and matching eyebrows. His eyes were light blue, identical to Peter's.

'Hello, boys, ready for two weeks of adventure?' Granddad asked, ruffling Peter's hair, and reaching out to shake George's hand.

'Can't wait to get there and show George the house.' Said Peter with a huge smile on his face. Jake barked from inside his crate, and Mrs Collins came round the car, hugged her dad and gave him a kiss on the cheek.

With Jake and the bags moved to Granddad's car it was time to set off for the Cove. Peter hugged his mum while getting a quiet final reminder not to tire out Granddad, and several kisses on the cheek.

Mrs Collins hugged her dad and waved them off from the car park. She always had a tear in her eye when her boy went off these first two weeks in summer. Some things never got easier.

As soon as they were on the road, Granddad began to tell George the stories about the Cove, and the legends that surrounded it.

'First-time visitors can be forgiven for thinking the Cove is just a small sleepy village with nothing much to offer and nothing to do.'

'Those people would be wrong. There is more to the Cove than meets the eye, that much you will see for yourself.'

'What's been happening lately Granddad?' asked Peter.

'Well, we have new neighbours for a start. Three sisters moved in next door, all very nice but keep themselves to themselves.'

'Apparently there were a group of amateur explorers who were heading for the Cove, but they've vanished. No trace of them or their cars. They were all booked to stay at the Inn but didn't show up, strange business.'

'They found another fossil in the woods, near the cove, huge this time. They think it might be a dragon.'

George and Peter exchanged bemused glances at this news. If Granddad was joking, he gave nothing away.

'Oh yes, they do say that in times gone by many dragons used to live in the woods, and in the vast caverns that are all around the Cove. Brave knights would come from all over to fight them. Many would lose, but for those few who killed a dragon, they were guaranteed immortality. Or so the story goes.' Granddad said looking at George, giving him a little nod of his head.

They drove in silence for a while and eventually the woods that surrounded one side of Campbell's Cove came into view. The road went through the middle of the woods, and when you were in there it was a little easier to believe the stories that Granddad had been telling. The trees blocked out nearly all the light and shadows danced everywhere. It was certainly not a place you would like to break down George thought to himself.

He stared into the trees and was sure he could see many strange shapes moving and following the car, just behind the tree line. Much to his relief, the darkness began to fade, and the car passed safely through the woods, and over the brow of a hill. There, in front of them, was Campbell's Cove. The sea looked enormous, spreading out from the edge of the land as far as the eye could see. In comparison, the Cove itself looked like the smallest town in the world to George.

They drove down the main street which was almost the only street in the village. There was one shop that also served as the post office. The news board outside the shop read 'Eggs go missing on several farms.' The boys looked at each other and laughed. There was only one bus stop outside the village hall, and across the road stood the Inn.

The main road was narrow with a small bridge halfway down which, when you crossed the road, much to George's amazement, got even narrower. There were houses in this part of the village; several small streets of five or six homes. All of which looked very much alike from the outside. Granddad turned off the main road and headed up a long sloping hill. There in front of them sat a row of four magnificent mansions. Each house was more impressive than the one before it.

'This one is ours.' Granddad said happily, as he looked at George, keen to see his reaction to the house.

They drove up to the house, and George's jaw dropped, sending Peter into fits of laughter. The large gates stood open revealing a sweeping driveway, and at its top the biggest house George had ever seen. The mansion had so many windows it seemed impossible to count.

The lawn was larger than five football pitches, and the trees that lined the edges looked like they had been plucked straight from the woods. As the car neared the house, George spotted two red squirrels playing chase on one of the trees, and a rabbit running across the lawn. The squirrels stopped as the car drove by, lifting their heads as if to say hello.

The rabbit was joined by two friends who also watched the car, then bounded off down the lawn. Jake started to bark, eager to get out and let the chase begin with the rabbits and squirrels, which he had never managed to catch. If truth be known, he probably never would.

The car finally reached the light-coloured gravel parking area, and everyone got out. George stood looking up at the house even more impressed with the size now that he was standing next to it. He turned, looking down the lawn, and could see a boy and girl coming up the drive on their bikes. They rang their bells, shouting Peter's name, waving as they got closer.

'It's Charlotte and James,' Peter said. 'They live down the road, and they come with me when I go exploring. They're my best friends in the Cove.'

Granddad busied himself emptying the car, putting the cases and bags up next to the impressive double front doors. Jake was finally let out of his cage and darted off down the lawn looking for rabbits to chase.

Charlotte and James dropped their bikes down beside the car and came over to say hello to Peter and be introduced to George.

James had blonde hair with blue eyes, and his sister had long light brown hair and bright green eyes with freckles on her nose.

'Hi, George I'm Charlotte, pleased to meet you.'

George tried to speak, opening his mouth to say hi or anything at all but no sound came out. His jaw dropped for the second time that day, and butterflies danced in his stomach. Charlotte was beautiful, and George had a hard time talking to beautiful girls.

'H-i-i.' He managed to stutter, going redder by the second.

Before the situation could get any more embarrassing, Granddad saved the day, announcing it was time for George to go on the grand tour.

Jake was oblivious to the embarrassment currently being suffered by George as he hunted, without success, for rabbits around the lawn. Suddenly he froze. The hair on the back of his neck rose, and a low growl began deep in his belly. Slowly he backed away then turned and ran at full speed back to his master.

It viewed the scene at the entrance to the mansion house and wondered who the visitors were. The dog was getting closer and closer. Just for fun it jumped from the tree, silent and unseen by the humans, and landed only feet from the dog. The dog sensed the danger and ran. It would have a closer look at the new arrivals later, but for now, it had work to do, work that couldn't wait. Silently it rose up into the air and moved away.

Chapter 3

Everyone, including Jake, gathered in the hall of the mansion. The suitcases and bags were lying in a bundle just inside the door. Granddad picked up the one he had asked for and moved it to the side. The hall was bigger than most houses with a magnificent staircase rising from the centre that split in two directions halfway up.

The walls were lined with expensive looking artwork, and in line with the bottom of the staircase, against each banister, stood two suits of knight's armour. Complete with shields and swords. There were several doors on either side, all hiding rooms just waiting to be explored.

The wooden floorboards were darkly polished, and the biggest rug you could imagine sat at the foot of the stairs. On the rug a large dragon was elegantly woven in dark red, standing next to a deep green forest. The dragon looked less elegant as Jake ran to the rug and rolled around on his back.

The children all laughed, and Charlotte went to get him off the rug which, of course, meant she was next in line for a face licking.

'Get off me you silly dog.' She shouted while laughing, trying to put Jake down without hurting him.

'Let the tour begin.' Granddad said, ushering everyone to gather round. Although the others had seen the house many times, they enjoyed hearing Granddad talk about it.

'We shall as always, work our way door to door on this floor, first making our way down the left-hand side then up the right-hand side. We will leave the basement till last as the best things are always left till last.' As he said this, he looked at George and winked.

'What's in the basement?' asked George.

'All in good time my lad,' Granddad replied with a smile.

The rooms down the left-hand side started with a huge library that had bookshelves from floor to ceiling packed with more books than George had ever seen. There were several tables with chairs placed around them, and two large armchairs by an even larger fireplace.

On either side of the fireplace stood stone statues that Granddad explained were gryphons; mythical beasts of times long forgotten rather like the Cove's own dragons.

'Where did you get them?' asked George.

'I believe this pair came from Egypt. A remarkable find in an old market if I remember correctly'.

'There are other works throughout the house that I hope you will find equally impressive,' Granddad continued, looking out one of the windows. He seemed to go into a dream for a moment then returned to move the tour on.

'Onwards now, onwards, we have lots to see.' Granddad said, leading the giggling children out of the room. Jake barked and ran around Granddad as if to show his approval.

The next room was Granddad's study, not a very impressive or interesting room for children, but to Granddad it was the best room in the house. The large oak desk was covered entirely with maps, books and drawings which he claimed were in perfect order but looked nothing of the sort.

There were more bookshelves behind the desk and a fireplace with no statues but another round rug. This rug showed a great bear rearing up as if ready to fight. There was also a globe, but when George looked closely, he realised that the place names were not recognisable, and the shapes of the continents looked different.

'Where's this globe from?' He asked, with a puzzled look on his face.

'Ah now, this globe is of a world that once was and is no more, apart from in the minds of few and memories of fewer.' Granddad said.

'What?' George asked.

Granddad chose not to answer and instead just tapped his finger twice against his nose then winked. The tour moved on.

'You'll get used to that.' Whispered Charlotte to George as she walked past him, flashing a smile that made him go red.

The next room was more like it for the children, the games room. A pool table, a table tennis table, and a TV with a DVD player and lots of films to watch.

'You see Peter, your old Granddad has finally replaced the video recorder.'

'Well, it was about time, no one has tapes anymore.' Peter said with a laugh.

There were no statues or rugs in this room, but there was a magnificent painting that took up almost the whole wall above the fireplace. In the picture, three knights battled a large ogre on the side of a river, with a burning village in the background.

'You do have a lot of odd statues and pictures around.' George said almost to himself.

'You may find that you grow to appreciate them more and more as the holiday goes on.' Granddad said from behind George. They both stared at the painting for a few seconds more before moving on.

The tour continued through the rooms on the ground floor. The biggest kitchen George had seen was followed by a large dining room and a living room with comfy sofas and beanbags that were so out of place with the rest of the house.

The final room on the ground floor took them back towards the front door. In this room, there was a wall for coats and hats, with shoes all over the floor. On the far wall, several television screens were showing different views outside the house.

All the screens had little green lights below them letting everyone know that everything was ok in that sector. The security system seemed a little over the top for such a small village as Campbell's Cove. The last screen showed a dark tunnel.

'Where's that?' George asked.

'That is where we will go to last.' Granddad replied.

They were each asked to grab a piece of luggage and anything else that needed to come to the bedrooms as the tour moved upstairs. They went up the stairs and turned left where they split in two. This took them on to a smaller flight of stairs, and then a corridor which ran all around the top floor and back down the stairs at the other side.

The first room would be Peter's as this was the room he always used when he stayed here. They quickly dropped in his bags and moved on to the next room which would be George's. It was much the same as Peter's with a single bed and a writing desk with two chairs at it.

There was also an armchair next to the large window. Above the writing desk was another painting; this time of a knight who seemed to be looking off into the distance while drawing his sword as if an enemy was approaching. The way the painting was hanging it looked as though the knight was staring directly at the bed.

The next two rooms were spare rooms, one of which was locked. Then a large bathroom with a ceramic dragon in the tiles. Granddad's room was next, but they didn't go in there. Then one more spare room, and what Granddad referred to as a reading room.

The reading room was a smaller version of the library with more sofas and chairs for comfort while reading. A large eagle was painted into the ceiling in stunning detail, its wings wide as it soared over them all.

Granddad led them back down the stairs at the other side leaving just one place to visit.

'Now we go to the basement!' exclaimed Granddad with pride in his voice.

Jake barked, and the other children smiled, and a buzz went between them.

'You're going to love this, George.' Said James as the group headed off towards the basement.

'What makes it so good?' asked George.

'You're about to see something you will not believe.' Peter said, building the suspense.

As they got to the bottom of the stairs, Granddad led the group right and stopped halfway along what looked like a solid wall with an ornate light fitting attached to it. Granddad pulled the light fitting down, and a hidden door opened under the stairs.

'Wow, cool.' George said, looking very impressed.

'Ha-ha, that always gets people the first time.' Granddad laughed. 'But wait till you see what's down here.' He said, picking up the suitcase Peter's dad had looked out for him.

'I'm going to need this.' He said with a satisfied look on his face.

Jake barked and ran off through the doorway that had appeared in front of them.

*****

Just as the children were entering the basement, a very different group entered the mouth of the biggest cave in Campbell's Cove. They used no torches or lights of any sort, though they walked easily in the dark, moving freely and with speed. Deeper and deeper into the caves they went finding passageways and openings that would not be visible to anybody else.

Finally, they came to a solid looking wall and stopped. The Master withdrew a large staff from inside their long black robe and tapped twice on the wall, muttering something quietly as they did. A small spark of orange light appeared next to the staff and slowly spread across the rock wall. The light formed the shape of a door, then with a loud grumbling noise the door shifted backwards and sideways revealing a huge cavern.

Inside the door two ogres stood guard, both moving instantly with bowed heads as the Master approached. Even these large beasts were terrified of the Master. They dared not look up until the group passed and the door was shut.

Below them, the cavern floor was a hive of activity with trolls and goblins and other unspeakable creatures working feverishly. As the group's presence became known a hush descended on the floor and the work stopped. The head troll came to greet the group and bowed low in front of them.

'Greetings, it is good to see you. As you can see, we have been making progress. We are working hard for you Master.' Graff spoke with a rough tone and his lips smacked at the end of every sentence. His tongue flicked out his mouth as he spoke.

'When do you expect it to be finished?' The Master asked, not hiding the disdain in their voice.

'Three more nights and we will be ready Master.'

'Excellent work Graff. I trust we have not encountered any problems?'

The slight hesitation from Graff, before answering, gave him away.

'Graff?' the Master said a question thick in their voice.

'We did have a slight problem with some humans almost discovering this place. They were exploring the caves. Don't worry though Tolldruck got them before they saw anything.' Graff began to smile. His lips cracked, and wrinkles appeared all over his face.

With a flash of movement, the Master reached out and grabbed Graff by the throat, lifting his grotesque form off of the ground with ease. Warts and spots popped and burst under the grip.

'If someone comes looking for them, and it brings them here Tolldruck will have a troll for dinner. Do I make myself clear?' The Master tightened their grip on his green slimy neck, and crushed the breath from the troll, only letting go when Graff was ready to pass out.

'Do not disappoint me again Graff. Once this phase is finished come and let me know. We have much planning to do.'

Without another word the group turned and walked back the way they had come. Although if you looked closely, you would see that no feet were touching the ground.

Chapter 4

The children followed on behind Granddad as he started after Jake. As they passed through the hidden door, lights came on along both walls illuminating a long passage that sloped gently downwards. Jake could be heard barking in the distance as they made their way further down.

'This is huge, where does it lead?' George asked, quickening his pace to draw level with Peter's Granddad.

'You are about to find out my boy.'

The tunnel ended at a flight of stairs, the air had become cold, and George swore he could hear water. They descended the stairs, and Granddad asked them all to stand together at the bottom until the lights came on.

'This is going to blow your mind.' James said to George.

'You will not believe this.' Charlotte added.

The lights came on in sections, revealing the most staggering sight George had ever seen. They were standing in an underground harbour built into a huge cavern. There, right in front of them, rocking slowly on the water was a Viking Longship. Perfect in every detail, and the sight was so unexpected that George stumbled into Peter in shock. Jake barked as the other children looked on laughing.

'What the... how is that possible... where did you... is that real?'

'Ha-ha, my boy. It is indeed real. I got it from Norway some time ago. I have been restoring it for years.' Granddad said with obvious pride in his voice as he looked on at his work.

'One day I will take her out into the sea, and she can regain her former glory as one of the queens of the waves.'

'How could you take that out to sea?' George asked. 'You would need loads of people to work all those oars.'

Granddad turned to George and winked but offered no answer to his question.

George tried again to take in his surroundings. On the wall to the right, he saw a large mural of what looked like the same Longship with a full crew of Vikings rowing her through a vicious sea.

'This Longship is called a Karvi.' Granddad explained, tapping George on the shoulder, pointing to the gang plank where everyone else was already walking onto the ship.

'A Karvi is the smallest Longship that the Vikings built and was used for military and trading. This one has been modified slightly making it longer and wider.'

As Granddad spoke, he withdrew a set of keys from his pocket and fiddled with them until he found the correct one. He unlocked the padlock on the suitcase he had carried down with him. Inside the case was another metal case with a key code lock on it. Granddad thought for a moment then keyed in the number, and the case opened.

'Ah, excellent. Come and gather round children.' Granddad said.

'It looks like a big piece of folded cloth.' Peter said, clearly disappointed by the contents of the case.

'It's the only Longship sail that has ever been found. This sail you are looking at is worth more than this house, and possibly more than the whole of Campbell's Cove.'

'Really? It can't be. It's just cloth.' Charlotte said.

'It came from the 10th century and was preserved in ice off the coast of Finland for most of its life. If it weren't for that ice, this cloth would have been long gone by now.'

With Granddad explaining what to do the children helped him fix the sail to the mast. With a triumphant smile, he gently hoisted the sail up, and they all watched it unfurl.

'She's almost entirely restored now. She just needs a bit more work on this damage here, and she'll be ready.'

He continued. He walked over to the front of the ship and examined the ornamental front piece, which was cracked and splintered. The children stayed on the ship for a while exploring it all before heading back up to the house.

With the tour finally over, and the children back upstairs Charlotte and James said their goodbyes and arranged to come back the next day.

'I still can't believe what I've just seen. That was amazing, staggering and unbelievable. Do you really think you can take it out to sea?' George asked.

'Oh yes and soon, I believe it will be very soon, maybe even within the next two weeks.' Granddad replied with a smile.

The boys followed Granddad into the kitchen where they sat and ate sandwiches and homemade soup. After not very much persuading, Granddad told more stories about the history of the Cove. He told one story of a Viking warrior who came from far away to slay one of the Campbell's Cove dragons.

'The story goes that the Viking arrived not by horse but by ship and came right into the cove with other Vikings as his companions. He marched to the church and declared to the minister that he would banish the dragons once and for all. His prize would be immortality.'

'Is that why you are interested in Viking ships?' George asked.

'It's part of the reason undoubtedly.' He replied, before continuing the story. 'After receiving a map from the minister, the brave warrior set off with fifteen Vikings at his side. His armour shone, and the whole village came out to cheer him on as he made his way through the town.

The dragon that had been causing the most problems was a massive beast the locals had named Tanis. She was huge, with red and black markings, and had destroyed countless farms and killed many brave knights who had taken up her challenge. It was believed she had two sons who were blamed for the killing of livestock, and the taking of children in the area.'

The food was forgotten as the story continued, and the two boys became more and more enthralled in the tale. It was one that Peter had not heard before. Maybe Granddad had been saving it for George's visit Peter thought.

'The warrior and his companions followed the map deep into the woods. As they got closer to where the minister had drawn his crude X on the page, the atmosphere changed. They noticed that there was no sound. No birds were singing, and no animals were moving across the woodland floor. Things had become very still.' Granddad looked at the boys, pleased to see them hanging on every word.

'Without warning, the ground in front of them opened up and a huge black and red dragon burst through grabbing a screaming Viking in its mouth, throwing him effortlessly through the trees. A swish of its tail sent another Viking crashing into some rocks, quickly chased by deadly fire from the beast's mouth.' Grandad was animated now, enjoying the role of storyteller.

'The Viking warrior did not panic; he lowered his sword and took two throwing daggers from his belt. He waited as the dragon turned to face the remaining men. The ground shook as the dragon reared up and roared. The wings unfolded, and it lifted, with ease, off the ground in a terrifying display of size and strength.' Grandad paced around the kitchen as he continued.

'The warrior saw his chance and skilfully aimed his daggers at the only soft spot on the underside of the dragon. The daggers were thrown so fast the beast had no time to move, and both struck the unprotected spot. A mammoth roar, and one last aimless blast of fire, and the dragon crashed to the ground with such force all the men were knocked off their feet. Dusting themselves down, they congratulated their hero.'

Granddad paused and drank some tea. His mouth was seemingly dry from the telling of such a tale. After some moments he continued.

'The group's joy at having killed the dragon soon left them when a fierce roar shook them to their very bones. They looked above them and caught glimpses of one of the other dragons through the treetops. Spears and long swords were readied as the Vikings got into formation with their leader. He dropped the front down on his helmet and took the bow and one solid silver arrow from his back.' Grandad made a motion as if he was stringing the bow.

'A double attack came quick as lightning, and dread passed through the men as the first dragon to attack was the same size as the one they had killed. It took two men in its claws as it swooped down on them then disappeared above the trees again. They could hear the screams of their fellow Vikings high above them.' Grandad looked upwards and the boys did the same.

'With a streak of movement from the other side, a massive dragon smashed through the trees and let out a flame so large five more men disappeared into smoke in seconds. The other dragon returned and landed next to its mother, roaring in unison so loudly the Vikings feared they would go deaf. The smaller one raced at the group.' George looked at Peter in disbelief, then back to Granddad, who continued.

'The Viking warrior held his nerve, waiting for the mouth to open before firing one silver arrow into the beast's throat. A roar of pain and the dragon reared up; he took his chance and shot the next arrow into the unprotected soft underbelly. The dragon staggered then crashed to the ground knocking over trees as it fell.'

The boys were gripped now, hanging on every word.

'Tanis, huge and powerful, roared in rage at what she had seen. She turned to face the group, focusing on the leader. She seemed to be sizing him up, looking for a weakness in this man who had slain her sons. The dragon really was huge, forty feet long, a twenty-foot tail and a wingspan wider than this house.' Grandad shook his head, as if even he could not believe his own story.

'Slowly it moved towards the men never taking its eyes off the warrior, keeping her weak spot hidden and never opening her mouth wide enough to allow an arrow to be used. Huge fangs were visible, and the horns on the dragon's head were at least six feet long. She stalked around the men patiently waiting for her chance.' Grandad walked slowly around the boys as he said this.

'A scream and a charge from one of the Vikings gave her that chance, and she swiped him away with a flash of her tail. Tanis charged the remaining men, stomping one and flicking another into the air effortlessly with her snout, opening her mouth long enough to eat the man whole. The other Vikings threw their spears and tried in vain to fight back, but one by one the dragon killed them all until only one remained.' He held up one long bony finger to emphasis the point.

'The beast turned towards the Viking warrior just in time to take the last silver arrow in the eye. She howled in pain, breathing fire towards him as he rolled quickly out the way. Even so, his armour saved him from a severe burning. Tanis took to the sky, and flames shot from her mouth burning trees all around the Viking, forcing him to run and head for cover deeper into the woods. The flames kept coming, and he ran until the woods cleared, and he found himself standing with the trees behind him and the water in front of him.'

'Looking around he could see a small beach with just a group of rocks and one bare tree for cover. The dragon had cleverly forced him into the open. He took off his helmet, to give him better vision, which was a risk but one he had to take. With no arrows or daggers left he drew his sword and circled slowly, looking for any sign of the dragon, keeping his shield high.'

'As the fight had gone on with the dragons, night approached almost unnoticed. The darkening sky and the setting sun hindered the Viking as he searched for her. He kept catching movement, a large dark shape circling overhead. The dragon swooped blasting fire at the Viking who got his shield up just in time and swung blindly with his sword. The heat of the flames scorched his skin and singed his hair.' Grandad touched his own hair as he said this.

'The dragon landed on the small beach and stared across confidently, stalking its prey with seeming contempt. He glimpsed over his shield and found himself looking straight into the dragon's one remaining eye. He looked to his side and saw the burning branches on the tree. The dragon charged, and the Viking knew he had only one chance.'

'He threw down his shield and ran as fast as he could towards the burning tree, grabbing one of the fallen branches. With the dragon almost upon him, he turned, and took aim, throwing the branch right into the dragon's good eye. The dragon howled in pain and took to the sky, blinded.'

Peter and George sat motionless as the story continued.

'In desperation the dragon began blasting fire randomly all over the beach, trying to hit the prey it could no longer see. A scream pierced the night and Tanis roared. The fire had hit the target. She landed, and breathed deeply sniffing out the fallen Viking, searching for his body. She finally found it near the rocks.' The boys looked visibly shocked, had the dragon won?

'Tanis pushed at the armoured boots with her snout. The Viking leapt out from his hiding place, and with one mighty swing he cut off Tanis's head as she inspected the empty boots. Exhausted, the Viking warrior dragged the head back through the wood and town to the church.'

'The people of the town were inside praying that their nightmare would end. They cheered when they saw him, and he was given a hero's welcome and treated like royalty. The next day, as had been promised, the minister and the town elders performed a ceremony that granted the Viking immortality.

'What happened then Granddad?' Peter asked.

'If he were granted immortality, wouldn't he still be here?' added George.

'That's a story for another day boys. Now eat up your dinner and you can spend some time in the game room before bed.' With that Granddad got up and left the kitchen and went to his study.

The boys finished their dinner then played pool for a while, chatting about the story and the fantastic first day. George couldn't stop talking about the Longship and couldn't wait to tell everyone back home what he had seen. After a couple of hours, the boys headed for bed and could see the light was still on in the study. Peter told George it was always best to leave Granddad alone when he was working in there.

Silently and gracefully, it moved unseen towards the mansion; it was time for a closer look at the new arrivals. The house itself was enough to make it curious, and the old man that lived there reminded it of someone.

It floated up towards the windows where it could hear the boys chatting to one another. Nothing unusual there, so why did this place make it uneasy? The yappy little dog was on one of the beds already asleep. It had enjoyed its bit of fun earlier on the lawn.

It moved down to the ground floor, and there was the old man sitting at his desk writing and looking at maps. What are you doing old man? It wondered as it watched him. There was something about him, about this place, all was not as it seemed here.

The Master will want to know its concerns, it was certain about that but not yet; not until the main project was finished. It didn't dare disturb the Master while the work was still on-going. It had other jobs to do, and other errands that needed to be completed. The Master's vision was almost complete, and soon they would be ready. Soon it would get to have all the fun it wanted.

Chapter 5

The boys woke early the next morning, something which did not please Jake. They were dressed and downstairs before 8 am and found Granddad already in his study.

'Have you been here all night?' asked Peter.

'Don't be silly Peter, some of us get up early you know. So, what is it to be today boys, some exploring of the caves or the woods perhaps?'

'I'd like to see the caves. If that's ok? Peter talks about them all the time. I can't wait to see them.'

'Very well, the caves it is. I assume Charlotte and James will be joining us for the adventure?' Granddad asked Peter, with one eye on George to see the reaction when he mentioned Charlotte's name.

Peter explained that he had sent James a text earlier and that they would be at the house around 10 am. George couldn't hide a smile as he realised they would be spending the day with Charlotte. He was excited but terrified of having to talk to her at the same time.

They ate breakfast; the smell of sausages convinced Jake to get up. After they had eaten, the boys took Jake for a walk out to the tree lined back garden which was roughly the size of two football pitches. A gravel path ran around the outside. There were several benches and a beautiful fountain made of shimmering grey stone that Peter said was granite.

The fountain was a sculpture of a man holding a bowl above his head. The water poured from the bowl down to his feet, splashing onto the pebbles at the bottom, and disappearing into five rectangular holes in the base.

The fountain didn't interest Jake, but the trees and bushes certainly did. He seemed very interested in the large hedge which separated the garden from the one next door, where the three sisters lived.

He spent a long time probing and looking for a way through, growling and barking then running further down and trying again. Daft dog, thought Peter, as he watched Jake run around in a seemingly aimless fashion.

The boys chatted about the caves, and Peter told George everything he could think of about the ones he had already seen. George managed to ask several questions about Charlotte and James and hoped that it was not too obvious he was only interested in the part of the answer that involved Charlotte. Jake finally found a way through the hedge, and the boys chased desperately to try and stop him.

'Jake, Jake come back boy!' shouted Peter as he raced down to where Jake had squeezed through. They could hear Jake on the other side of the hedge, barking and growling. Peter hoped that no one was home.

Suddenly all the noise from the other garden stopped, they couldn't hear Jake barking or moving around. The boys exchanged puzzled looks and started shouting for the dog.

As there were still no noises coming from through the hedge, Peter ran back up to get Granddad while George stayed in case Jake came back through. George tried to see through the gap and knelt down putting his hand through while continuing to call for Jake. His hand brushed against something furry, that felt like Jake, so he tried to grab on but was shaken free.

'Jake, come back right now.' He shouted, but again there was no sound.

Peter reached the house to find Granddad standing at the front door talking to a very tall old woman who was holding Jake. The lady had a stern face, with a long nose and large mouth. Her black hair was tied back exposing a pale white forehead. Unusually Jake wasn't trying to lick her face or wriggle himself free.

'I am very sorry, I thought there were no holes in that hedge, but Jake always manages to find one that I miss.' Granddad was saying as Peter came up to them. Jake barked, and the woman let him go. Jake ran straight to Peter, jumping into his arms. Peter stroked him calming him down.

'Peter, you must keep a better eye on Jake, and not let him run through to the neighbours.' Granddad said.

'I'm sorry.' Peter said to both Granddad and the old lady. He looked confused and stared at her as he spoke.

'How did you get here so quick?' Peter asked. 'Jake only went through the hedge a couple of minutes ago.'

'I am sure you must be mistaken about that.' Granddad said looking first at Peter then at Ms Kirke.

'It is not as if I could run round here at the speed of light, or fly over the hedge now, is it?' she said with a laugh. Her voice was soft and soothing and did not suit such a stern face.

Just then George came running into the room to tell Peter about almost catching Jake.

'Peter I almost got... oh there he is, I thought I just caught hold of him through that gap.'

'It won't happen again Ms Kirke, I will see to that.' Granddad said apologetically.

'Boys will be boys and dogs will be dogs, Mr Thornton. I am just glad he didn't get hurt. That back garden is a dangerous place until we can get all our work finished.'

They said their goodbyes and Ms Kirke headed down the path.

Both boys looked at her with the same expression on their faces.

'What is it, boys?' asked Granddad.

'There's no way she could have gotten here so quickly with Jake.'

'That's exactly what Peter said when he saw her.' Granddad replied. 'Interesting, very interesting indeed. However, it is a mystery that will have to wait for another time. Here come your friends and it's time to go exploring.' Granddad said, pointing down the path to where Charlotte and James had just come into view.

As the children all said hello, Peter and George told their story about Jake and Ms Kirke. Granddad went to the kitchen to fetch the backpack with the provisions for the first day of exploring. Just as he entered the kitchen, he was sure he caught a glimpse of movement by the window, not much, just a glimmer, but it was there.

'Things are getting very interesting around here.' Granddad said to himself glancing out the window one last time before heading to join the children and Jake.

They walked through the town, down the hill to the main street, past the shop and village hall. They walked by Charlotte's school then took a turn down an almost hidden path that led directly to the beach.

The beach was a mixture of sand and stones with a strong smell of seaweed in the air. The water was calm, and there was a slight breeze. Granddad led the way along the beach towards the caves. He was unusually quiet and didn't tell any of his stories about sea monsters, dragons or the creatures that hide deep in the caves.

'Is everything ok?' Peter asked.

'What? What? Eh, oh yes, I'm sorry I was miles away there, lost in thoughts of long ago. I've not been a very good tour guide at all this morning; let me put that right straight away.'

He turned to the children motioning for them to stop.

'George, did you know that the cave we are going to see today is rumoured to be home to a terrible sea creature?' he asked.

'Emm, no I didn't.' Replied George, with a quizzical look, as he wondered where this story was going to go.

'If you take the time, as I have, to learn the history of the Cove down through the centuries you see several stories repeat themselves every so often. One such story is of a giant sea monster that lives in the underground lakes and pools of the caves.' Grandad pointed down the beach towards the caves.

'Unlike the dragons it was never killed, many tried, but no one came close. No knight or brave soul who entered the caves to meet the beast ever returned.' Granddad was in full swing now and glimpsed at George to see his reaction. George was looking nervously between Granddad and the cave.

'Oh, don't worry George we're not going that deep into the Cave. It is rumoured that the beast lives in the deepest pool in the furthest part of the cave from the surface. I have read many accounts of it, and there have been no sightings or new stories of the monster for the past one hundred years.'

The children looked at each other and smiled. George let out a nervous laugh. Granddad was such a good storyteller they were never sure whether he was serious or not. They reached the cave with Granddad leading the way. He stopped at the mouth, placed his bag on the ground, and took out torches which he passed to the children. He clipped a lead on to Jake, which Jake was not pleased with.

He reminded them all to stay close and look out for each other. Everyone turned on their torches and entered the cave. It was quite small, to begin with, but soon the roof of the cave rose up while the floor sloped gradually down.

The torch beams searched through the semi-darkness giving glimpses of smooth wet walls, and the occasional bat flying overhead. There were small pools of water dotted here and there. Ripples of movement could be seen in some of them.

'Nothing to worry about just drips from the roof splashing in the pools.' Granddad said, raising his torch upwards towards the wet, shimmering roof of the cave.

'These caves are often explored by lots of visitors. As long as you obey the rules and stay close to the surface then you should steer clear of any sea monsters or cave creatures.' Granddad said with a smile while casting his torch around. It never failed to amaze him how big these caves were.

The children were enjoying themselves, jumping from one rock to another, leaping over the pools and helping each other along the way. George was the least sure-footed having never been in a cave before, and although he would not admit it probably the most nervous one of the group.

As the cave turned a corner, George looked round and noticed that the entrance was no longer visible. He let his torchlight dance off the walls as he turned to join the others, and there, just at the edge of the beam, he was sure he saw something move. Bigger than a bat, much bigger, it seemed to dart away from the light.

Trick of the light George decided, and just as he was about to rush on to join the others, a large splash came from a pool below where he had seen the shape. George froze unsure what to do or whether to shout out. He had made up his mind to move when a hand suddenly gripped his arm. George screamed; jumping backwards he fell onto his backside, and his torch rolled away from him.

'George I'm sorry, I didn't mean to scare you, you were falling behind, and I wanted to make sure you were ok.' The hand that had gripped him belonged to Charlotte. George was happy for the semi-darkness as he was sure it would hide his blushing cheeks.

'It's ok, I am fine, I wasn't scared, I just err... I just em... well I lost my footing and slipped that's all.' George got himself back to his feet and grabbed his torch. He walked with Charlotte to join the others who were waiting by a larger pool.

'It's ok George; everyone gets scared the first time they come into the caves. What were you doing?' asked Granddad.

'I thought I saw something near the roof of the cave, and then there was a big splash in one of the pools.' George said telling the truth but feeling foolish at the same time.

'There are lots of things in these caves George that will do you no harm but do not like the light. They will try and avoid the light as we try to avoid the dark places,' Granddad said reassuring George.

'The first time we came down here both Peter and I slipped and fell in one of the shallow pools.' James added.

'We were trying to look for fish, and I leant too far over and fell; grabbed on to James taking him with me.'

The children continued to laugh and joke lightening the mood, and George forgot all about his embarrassment. The only one not laughing was Granddad. He moved back slightly and cast his torch towards the roof of the cave where George said he had seen something move. He then brought the beam down to the pool where the splash had come from. Something moved away from the light just under the surface. Jake gave out a low growl and pulled on the lead. He was pulling to get away from the pool, though, not to investigate it further.

'It appears we are not alone.' Granddad said to himself before turning and joining the children.

It had almost been seen; this just would not do. It was not supposed to come this close to the surface, not yet. Graff had been very clear. Stay deep in the cave and if any humans came near it was to watch them, and if they got too close, it was to come back and report what was going on.

It would be Graff who would decide if Tolldruck should be sent to take care of unwanted visitors. After the Master's visit Graff had become more nervous. It liked to explore the caves, but this had been a warning.

Luckily it was just some children and an old man, old by human standards. The dog seemed harmless enough. It watched the group move away then silently, with great care, it rose out the pool and crept along the walls back to the cave roof. It made its way past them and scurried off deeper into the caves. If they came too close, it would report back to Graff. Otherwise, it would say nothing. Graff might feed it to Tolldruck for disobeying his orders.

Chapter 6

They stopped after another twenty minutes next to the largest pool they had seen so far. There was a big flat rock where they all gathered to look out onto the pool, which could easily have been called a lake. A faint light cast a soft glow over the water.

'We shall have some sandwiches here then head back; this is far enough for today.' Said Granddad, beginning to undo his backpack and pass out food to the children. Jake sat patiently waiting for his travel bowl to appear.

'Don't worry boy I've not forgotten you.' Granddad said to Jake putting the bowl down next to him. Jake buried his head as far in as he could go, eating noisily.

The children ate their sandwiches and drank the juice from the flask Granddad had brought with him.

'Can I ask a question about the Viking in your story last night?' George asked, looking up from his sandwich.

'Of course, you can George, what is it?' replied Granddad, putting down his drink, looking very seriously towards George.

'Well, what happened once he was granted immortality, I mean, would he not still be around today?'

'George you are quite right, quite right indeed.' began Granddad. The children sensed the answer would be long, and all gathered round.

'For many years he lived right here in the Cove. He lived a hero's life. Rumour has it he fought witches and trolls in these very caves, winning every time. Even an immortal man has a weakness, though, and that weakness is also a great strength.'

'I'm lost.' Charlotte said, tilting her head to the side, raising a question with her expression.

'His weakness was love; falling in love to be precise.' Granddad looked out over the pool as he spoke, never looking at the children. 'You see some nine hundred years or so after he was granted his immortality, he met a woman called Melissa and fell in love. Over time she fell in love with him, and they spent many years together.' He paused and took a long drink before he continued.

'He went back to the church to speak to the only people who could help him and begged to be released from the spell and to grow old with Melissa.'

'After much deliberation, the church elders decided that the threat from dragons and other dark creatures had passed, and they granted the Viking his wish. A secret ceremony was performed, which removed the spell, and he became human again.'

'When was this, are they still alive?' asked Peter.

'The rumour has it that the Viking lives on, an old man now, but the stories tell us that Melissa died fifteen years after they were married in an accident out at sea. Her body was never recovered, but her small boat was found damaged and floating just a few miles out from the Cove.' Granddad paused before continuing.

'Love can give you such happiness, then can break the very heart it filled, leaving a hole that can never be fixed or protected by any armour.' Granddad appeared to have finished the story, and Peter could have sworn he saw a single tear run down his cheek.

The group ate their sandwiches and drank the rest of their juice in silence, thinking about the story they had heard. George moved over to the pool, he looked out across the water, listening to the waves echo in the cave. Charlotte got up and moved next to George, who was determined not to make a fool of himself this time.

'What was the story that Mr Thornton told you last night?' She asked.

George told Charlotte the story about the Vikings and the dragons, all be it a shortened version and not as dramatically told.

After George had finished Charlotte was quiet for a time seemingly thinking about something.

'It seems odd that Mr Thornton has just started talking about this Viking warrior now. I had never heard that story before, and he's told us hundreds in the past.'

'Maybe he was saving some good ones for my visit.'

Before they could discuss it any further Peter told them Granddad had decided it was time to head back home for the day.

*****

As the children and Granddad began their journey out of the caves, deep within them work was continuing under Graff's watchful eye. Graff was a vile looking creature. He was tall for a troll, and fat. His grey/green skin had a constant film of sweat, and his warts and spots spouted puss at regular intervals. His eyes were yellow with small pupils of purest black.

His hands looked more like claws, and his yellow and black teeth were broken and chipped. There seemed to be too many jostling for position in his mouth. His black tongue was covered in warts, which didn't bother him at all.

The work had reached a crucial point; enough eggs had been gathered by the shadow walkers to begin the final stage. Five huge vats of boiling water stood over white hot fires that were being stoked by goblins who didn't mind the heat. Their skin was so thick and tough the only fire that could penetrate it was dragon fire.

To the side of the vats stood a large hourglass which would be turned as soon as the eggs were released into the water. It was crucial that each and every egg was given the exact same time to boil to perfection. Over or under boiling would result in the Master being displeased, and almost without fail a goblin or two would be boiled to show just how unhappy the Master was.

The shells had to be perfect; not too hard but not too soft. Once this stage was over, they could complete their work, and at last, their plan could be put into action.

Graff climbed above the vats and could see the water boiling nicely. He shouted for the eggs to be released, and as soon as they hit the water the hourglass was turned. A smile spread on his hideous mouth as he thought of how pleased the Master would be with him once this was over. His creation would allow them to fulfil the Master's plan.

His black tongue flicked out over his cracked lips, licking pus away from the corner of his mouth. It had been centuries since he had looked forward to something so much. Graff shouted more orders, keeping his workers on their toes. They would all reap the rewards when the time comes, and Graff knew that time was approaching fast.

*****

As they walked back through the caves Granddad was very quiet; his face showed no expression, but his mind was running over the events of the day - Ms Kirke and her sudden appearance with Jake, the feeling he was being watched in the kitchen and the brief encounter in the caves. He was sure something was happening, maybe the very something he had been waiting and planning on for many years.

The children were his concern, Peter and George were staying at his house, and that meant that if he was right, they could be in danger. Once he was sure he would have to tell them, but not yet. He needed to be back at his study to do some more research and preparation. Even if he were wrong, it would not hurt to be ready. The children cheered as the mouth of the cave came into view, waking Granddad from his thoughts.

'Well, George how was your first trip into the Caves of Campbell's Cove?' Granddad asked as the children handed him back the torches.

'It was good, kind of weird with whatever it was splashing into the water, but fun as well. I enjoyed your story; can you tell us more later on please?'

'Oh, don't worry you'll hear more stories about the Viking, maybe even more about the witches and other creatures I mentioned as well. This little village hides many secrets and has many fine tales to tell.' Granddad smiled as the children all began to walk back up towards the village. He turned around and looked into the darkness of the cave.

'I know you are here somewhere.' He said to himself before setting off after the children with Jake by his side.

The children said their goodbyes at the bottom of Granddad's drive, and Charlotte told Peter and George that they would come round tomorrow. A smile spread across George's face as he heard this news. He stood watching Charlotte walk away and was caught staring when she turned round suddenly to wave one last time. He blushed and waved back then turned to walk up the drive. Just for a second, he was sure he saw a shape on the roof of the mansion. A shimmer in the sunlight, then it was gone.

Chapter 7

Graff looked on with great satisfaction. Finally, the work was complete. Goblins, trolls and other creatures stood admiring their work. Their bodies were hot and slimy with sweat and blood from the hard toil that had gone before. They had finished their task within the deadline set by the Master, which gave Graff an equal measure of pride and relief. Tolldruck would not be having a troll for dinner after all.

A cold shiver ran up his spine, causing the thick black hairs on his neck and back to stand up.

'A pleasant surprise Graff, a pleasant surprise indeed.' the Master said, appearing from nowhere.

'Our plans have been moved forward. We must be ready within one Earth day. We may have been discovered, and it would be best to act quickly and be gone.'

'We are ready Master, and we are eager to begin.' said Graff, his thick tongue flicking out as he spoke to lick pus from his cracked lips.

'Tomorrow, when night falls, we will begin. The shadow walkers have done their jobs, and we know where our targets are. There should be no problems.' Said the Master, and without another word turned and floated upwards before disappearing. No smoke, no big bang and no theatrics; just there then gone.

'You heard the Master, tomorrow our mission begins.'
Graff said triumphantly raising his arms. His workers
cheered and began preparing for the work ahead.

*****

*Something was odd, something about this place did not
seem right. It could not say exactly what it was, but
something made it feel uneasy when it went near the old
man's mansion. It watched him in his study where he
had been working for over an hour now.*

*The children were in another room playing some kind
of game. Mindless activities for mindless children, and
there with them was that awful dog. It floated back to the
study window and watched. Something it saw took it by
surprise; it can't be, can it? It must be mistaken, how is
that possible?*

*It went in for a closer look, right up to the window, and
now there was no doubt. The Master would want to
know this. It looked at the old man and was surprised to
find him looking straight back at it. Of course, he could
not see it, simply coincidence.*

*The old man smiled, then rose and closed the curtains.
Like a shot, it was off. The Master would want to know,
and the Master would know exactly what to do about it.*

He felt he was being watched but by what he could not
tell. Granddad was in his study finalising his work when
the realisation hit him. He looked to the window and

thought he caught the briefest of movements. He was sure he was right about being watched, and about what he felt was happening.

It would soon be time to tell the children, but how to tell them and what to say to them exactly. A glimmer of movement outside the window and now he was certain. He smiled, crossed the room and closed the curtains.

Granddad left the study but didn't go to the boys in the games room. Instead, he headed for the Longship. As the lights came on, he looked at the beautiful ship, running his hand along the glossy wood.

It wasn't quite ready for the sea yet, but maybe it would have to do. He climbed on board and counted out his paces until he came to the correct place. He moved his hand along the smooth wood releasing the hidden hatch. He removed the package, heavier than he remembered. Moving quickly back up to the main house he could not deny that he felt excited as well as nervous.

He found the boys still playing pool in the games room and asked them to come and join him in the kitchen for some dinner and another story. The boys gladly put down their cues and followed through to the kitchen. They sat in the same seats as before and were pleased to smell a pizza cooking in the oven.

'What story are you going to tell us, Granddad?' asked Peter.

'I am going to tell you another tale about the Viking warrior. Do you remember I mentioned that he had fought witches and goblins?' The boys nodded and looked on expectantly.

'Good, well then there is more to that story, and this is where we shall begin.'

'Several centuries after fighting and defeating Tanis and her sons, the immortal Viking was again summoned to the church after a group of children disappeared. They had been on a midnight summer walk with two church Elders who were also missing. There had been reports of loud roars through the night near the caves, and some villagers claimed to have seen fire light up the sky. It appeared the dragons were back in Campbell's Cove.' Granddad paused and took a long slow drink from the glass of water by his plate.

The boys had forgotten all about their drinks, and even the smell of pizza no longer seemed so interesting.

'He left the church and went straight to the caves taking the bravest and strongest men of the Cove with him. There were signs of a struggle outside the cave and lots of footprints, some human some not, which led inside. The Viking drew his sword leading the men deep into the caves. Torches were lit to see the way, and soon the group could hear noises ahead. They could hear the unmistakable roar of a dragon.'

'Some of the men were scared, and a couple turned and ran back the way they had come. No sooner had they run off than their screams could be heard echoing through the caves. Something was now behind the group, and there was no going back.' Granddad paused once again, this time, to remove the pizza from the oven.

The boys were amazed he could remain so calm during such an enthralling story. Their amazement did not stop either of them taking huge bites of the pizza. Jake patrolled the floor looking for any crumbs that came his way.

Granddad continued. 'The group doused their torches in the pools of water and continued on. Their fear of being seen outweighed their fear of what might lurk in the dark. Soon they were standing at the top of a basin within the cave. They crept to the edge and surveyed the scene below them. All kinds of unthinkable creatures scurried around carrying things here and there and guarding cages. There was a dragon, but it was in ropes, and its roars were the anguished roars of imprisonment. It had been caught by these creatures.'

'This is the best story you have ever told.' Peter said.

'Totally agree.' George added with his mouth full of pizza.

'Quietly the group made their way down towards the activity. Staying in the shadows, the Viking led them towards the cages and the dragon. There was so much going on down at the basin floor that their progress was never noticed. They got close enough to see into the cages and saw the children inside scared and huddled together. He asked his men to stay where they were and remain quiet and sneaked off without another word.' Granddad put his finger to his lips for effect.

'He went round the edge of the activity keeping low to the ground. His speed of movement amazed the others. Within seconds he was across the floor and close to the cages, but he didn't stop. Instead, he headed for the dragon. The dragon noticed the Viking approaching, watching him wearily. The Viking drew his hunting dagger as the helpless dragon looked on.'

'It was so tightly tied up all it could do was watch. He began to cut through the ropes one by one. The dragon did not move a muscle or roar or do anything to draw attention to what was happening. You see dragons are very intelligent animals, and this one recognised it was being freed. It would soon have the chance to get revenge on its captors.'

Granddad paused and took a bite of pizza. Crumbs showered the floor much to the delight of Jake.

'All the ropes were cut, and the dragon was free. It looked at the man who had set it free, and an understanding passed between them. The Viking snuck off behind the cages and spoke to the children. The dragon waited until two of his tormentors were close by before bursting free and blasting fire, turning them to ash in the blink of an eye.' Granddad clicked his fingers as he said this.

'With a deafening roar, it rose up to its full height and began to attack the goblins and trolls. The confusion gave the Viking the opportunity to free the children as the other men joined the fight. More and more goblins rushed into the basin, and the dragon blasted fire in every direction killing scores of them before they could draw their weapons. The men fought bravely, and soon the children were making their way up the basin back towards the entrance of the cave.'

'Keep going Granddad; you can't pause all the time.'

Granddad smiled and reached down to stroke Jake before going on.

'As the children began their escape the Viking joined the dragon in the fight against the goblins and trolls. Together they seemed unstoppable, and it looked like the fight would be won. Suddenly from above the children there was a deep booming roar. The goblins and trolls stopped attacking the Viking and stopped following the children and men.'

'Instead, they ran into the shadows and hid. Another roar and this time even the dragon hesitated, unsure as to what was approaching. Whatever it was terrified their enemies. The children and men ran back down and hid behind the dragon. A hooded figure appeared at the top of the basin and looked down upon the group. It stared directly at the Viking and began to speak.'

'You thought you could win this fight?' The figure asked. 'You thought you could come here and rescue these children? You thought wrong It said as it turned to look back towards the cave opening. 'It is time for you all to meet Tolldruck.'

'What's a Tolldruck Granddad?' asked Peter.

'There's only one Tolldruck, just as well as one is bad enough. He is a vile, evil beast, huge, powerful and utterly fearless with a cunning intelligence that takes his enemies by surprise.'

'What happened next? Did the Viking and children escape?' George spoke with his mouth full, and pizza fell towards the floor. Jake leapt into action catching the pizza and swallowing it in one movement.

'The roars grew louder as Tolldruck drew closer. Finally, they could see him. Twelve-foot tall, solid muscle and skin as black as the night. Red eyes with yellow slits for pupils stood out against the dark skin. Tolldruck growled at the group revealing razor-sharp teeth, and a thick black forked tongue. It stood upright like a man but had a strong tail that swirled and curled behind it, occasionally crashing off the cave floor. Its feet were huge and webbed. It had four arms covered in muscles, and each hand had thick talons at the end of every finger.' Granddad extended his own fingers curling them into claw shapes.

'Tolldruck roared and leapt from the ledge landing on the cavern floor perfectly balanced and ready to strike. Two of its arms planted on the ground, the other two raised. A wicked smile spread across Tolldruck's mouth as his huge teeth became visible. With incredible speed and strength, Tolldruck struck sending the dragon crashing back against the empty cages. The Viking and men got ready to fight as Tolldruck turned its attention to them. Arrows and daggers were thrown, all bouncing off with no effect.'

'Tolldruck laughed and swept forward grabbing a man in each of its four hands throwing them against the cavern walls. The Viking was fast enough to evade the attacks dodging out the way and striking with the sword when the chance arose. The sword seemed to be the only weapon that could cut the skin of this beast. He continued evading and countering as Tolldruck showed no signs of pain and kept the relentless attack going.'

'The Viking was tiring but fought on knowing that while Tolldruck was fighting him, it was not focusing on the children. The dragon regained its senses rising from the wreckage of the cages flying upwards before swooping towards Tolldruck, smashing into him and sending them both to the ground. A ferocious fight began between the two giants. The dragon blasted fire while Tolldruck clawed and swirled its strong tail, battering the dragon again and again.'

'Eventually, Tolldruck began to win the fight, picking up the dragon and throwing it against the wall where it fell still and silent. Tolldruck roared and ran across the cavern looking for the children. The Viking intercepted, but this time, Tolldruck was ready. He dodged out the way before smashing one strong arm into him sending the Viking to the floor. Tolldruck circled the children, laughing, licking his lips and taunting them. The remaining men charged but were defeated in seconds. The children were now defenceless against this beast.'

Granddad stopped and stared off out the window.

'What, wait you can't stop there, you just can't, what happened next?'

'Tolldruck was enjoying himself, feeding off the fear of the children. Just as he was about to move in the Viking appeared from nowhere, and with one mighty swipe took half of Tolldruck's tail off. Tolldruck roared in pain and surprise spinning to face the Viking just in time to see the dragon flying at him as fast as it could go. The dragon grabbed Tolldruck before he could react, lifting him up, flying higher until they both smashed through the cave ceiling. On and on the dragon flew holding on to Tolldruck ignoring his attempts to free himself. While the dragon was carrying off Tolldruck, the Viking gathered the children and began the climb out of the cavern.'

He paused for a drink before continuing.

'The hooded figure and all the trolls and goblins had vanished. The only sounds were now the sobbing of the children, and the voice of their rescuer reassuring them and guiding them on. They reached the entrance to the cave and ran out onto the beach. They saw a large ship crash out on the waves and speed away. A deadly storm brewed almost immediately, and the Viking had to rush the children back up to the village.'

'The villagers were happy to see their children return though saddened by the loss of so many men in such a short battle. Neither Tolldruck nor the dragon was ever seen again after that night. The large ship vanished and with it all trace of the monsters that were in the cavern. Nobody understood why they had come or where they came from, but the Viking always remained wary of their return.'

'Wow, what a brilliant story, but Granddad how do you know so much about all of this?' asked Peter taking another slice of pizza and a gulp of his juice.

'You could say it has become my life's work, it is what I do in my study all day, and I'm a keen historian of the Cove as you know.' Granddad said reaching down to pick up the package at his feet.

'It is why I want to show you this, and how I think you will believe that these stories are true, and not just the imagination of a crazy old man.' He said with a smile as the boys came closer to see what was inside the package.

The boys gasped as Granddad opened up the package very carefully and there in front of them, on the kitchen table, was a beautiful sword. The handle was a design of blended silver and gold, and the blade shone in the lights. There were scorch marks on the blade and a small piece missing near the tip.

'Is that what I think it is Granddad?'

'It is indeed. This is the sword of the Viking warrior, the sword that killed Tanis and injured Tolldruck. The sword that helped rid the Cove of the monsters and nightmares that kept families in fear.'

'How did you get it? How would you know where to begin looking for something like that?' George asked staring at the sword, reaching out to touch the handle.

'I have had many years to uncover the secrets of the Cove and to read through all the histories in the Church vault. The maps in my study helped me find the locations of many things and piece together several mysteries. It is because of my knowledge and the work I have done that I feel I now must tell you both something else.'

'Is it another story about the Viking Granddad?'

'Not this time Peter. This is about history, but it also affects right now. I think there may be something happening in the cove, something that has occurred in this area before.'

'What is it, what do you mean?' George asked.

'I told you that the Viking warrior originally arrived to help rid the Cove of the dragons that were causing so much destruction. This history of the dragons turning up and children, livestock and eggs going missing would repeat itself every one hundred years. It was when they found the dragon taken prisoner in the cavern the night they fought Tolldruck that they realised the dragons were not to blame.' He looked at the boys to make sure they understood before continuing.

'It was these other monsters that were responsible and made it look like the dragons were causing all the problems. The dragons would, of course, defend themselves when men tried to hunt them, so it made them enemies of each other. The men looked no further for anything else to blame; the dragons were the obvious culprits.'

The boys both nodded and urged Granddad to go on.

'After they had fought the battle in the cavern the men of the Cove went back to the caves and spent many days and nights exploring every inch of them. They found passages that had previously been unknown and whole caves that were unexplored. In these caves, they found evidence that the visitors had been here before. One of the discoveries was a full dragon skeleton still imprisoned in the chains.'

'They read over the history of the Cove and found that every one hundred years these things would happen, and the dragons would be blamed. They noticed that at the end of the activity there were always reports of a massive storm. After they had put all this together, the Viking vowed to be ready the next time. He trained the men of the Cove to fight when the time came. One hundred years later the Viking waited and waited, but the visitors did not return. It was decided by the church elders that what had happened the previous century had scared the monsters away. Without being able to blame the dragons they could not return unnoticed.'

'Is that why the church decided to grant his wish to be allowed to grow old?' Peter asked, remembering the story from the caves trip.

'Yes, it is Peter. They saw no need to have him remain immortal when the threat had been removed. It had been over one hundred and seventy years since anything had happened, so the Viking was released from the spell.'

'Why are you telling us this now Mr Thornton?' George asked.

'I am telling you because that fight in the caves took place two hundred years ago this week.' Granddad said looking at both boys in turn to gauge their reaction.

'Several things have happened recently that have made me think that something is wrong once again in the

Cove. A group of men who told their loved ones they were coming to the Cove to explore the caves have vanished. Thousands of eggs have been stolen from all over the surrounding area. George, you said you saw something in the caves when we were exploring. I saw it too; I caught a glimpse as it shied away from the light.'

'You saw it? Why didn't you say so at the time?' George said visibly relieved that someone else had seen something.

'Would it have benefited you? It was just one more piece of evidence for me that things are not as they should be.' Granddad replied.

'Do you think we are in danger Granddad?' Peter questioned.

'While you are in this house you are safe Peter, please trust me on that.'

'How can you be so sure?'

'Trust me, Peter, this old mansion is more secure than you could possibly imagine.'

'But why have eggs gone missing?' George asked.

'Let's all go to my study where I can answer that question and any others you have,' Granddad replied already moving towards the door.

When they got to the study, Granddad asked the boys to take a seat, as he took his behind the large desk. He shuffled through papers and maps and seemed to be sorting them out into an order.

'Let us start with the question you asked about eggs.' Granddad said, looking at George, as he took several pages of notes from a folder.

'There is an old Scottish tale that says witches used eggshells to make boats, as this was the only way they could travel over water. Although partly right I discovered, through years of research, that they used the eggshells to coat the bottom of their ships. They did this because there was something in the shells, once boiled, that they can use their magic on to create a storm so fierce very few vessels can follow them. This makes it easier for the witches to escape from places like the Cove.'

'Is that why a storm happened when the Viking freed the children?' Peter asked.

'Indeed, it is, and that was also the last time so many eggs went missing from the areas around the Cove, until now.'

The boys looked at each other as they began to realise what Granddad meant.

'Have the witches returned granddad?' Peter asked.

'It is my belief that they have Peter, it is also my belief that they may have been here for some time working in the deepest caves.'

'Are you not scared? I mean if they are here will they not try and attack the Cove and steal children; children like us?' George's voice shook as he asked the question.

'I am not scared for many reasons. Firstly, this mansion is not a place witches will find easy to get into. Secondly, if they do manage to get in, they might not get back out. Thirdly there is one boat that can follow any ship in a stormy sea with the greatest of ease. Do you know what that ship might be?'

The boys looked at each other, and then at Granddad who began to smile.

'A Viking Longship.' Peter said.

'Exactly. I have always thought that one day the witches would return, and I wanted to be ready when they did. Someone has to defend the Cove, and I have had one hundred and seventy years to prepare.' Granddad said then seemed to catch himself and stopped talking.

'What do you mean you have had one hundred and seventy years to prepare?' George asked.

'Just how old are you Granddad?' Peter added.

'Oh what, em no, I meant I had had one hundred and seventy years of history to read through, and plenty of time to collect the correct items to assist me should anything happen in the future.'

'What should we do if you are right? Shouldn't we call mum and let her know what you think?'

Granddad laughed. 'What do you think your mother would say if you told her that I thought the Cove was overrun with witches and monsters? She would have me in a care home before the week was out.'

'This must stay between us, and if I am right, we must prepare to defend the Cove as the Viking did all those years ago.'

'There is more to this mansion than meets the eye and you will learn that very soon, but for now you should both try and get some rest. The next few days could prove to be very tiring.'

'How can we sleep after hearing so many stories, and knowing we could be in danger?' George asked.

'George, you must trust me, you are in no danger while you are in my house.' Granddad said ushering the boys out of his study and up the stairs to their rooms.

George said goodnight to Peter and went into his room to get ready for bed. As he did, he stared at the painting of the knight and thought something was odd. He had not paid attention to it before, but he was sure the sword had changed position. George laughed at himself for being so silly and turned towards his bed. Just as he did this, the painting behind him moved ever so slightly.

Chapter 8

Charlotte and James were getting ready for bed in their house just off the main street. The house was situated on the water in a very picturesque part of Campbell's Cove. Charlotte looked out of her window and gazed at the night sky full of bright stars. She loved the night and the peace of the cove.

She enjoyed listening to the water, and the smell of the beach. Her thoughts turned to the cave adventure they had today and how silly George was. It was nice to see Peter again, and she liked George as well. Charlotte was looking forward to seeing them tomorrow, and also to finding out what Peter's Granddad had planned for them.

She left the curtains open and turned off the light. Her room became dark, although the moonlight cast a soft glow across her bed. She thought it was odd that the light from the moon did not reach the far corner of her room or the ceiling where she had her own stars that glowed in the night.

One patch of the stars was not glowing; in fact, they didn't seem to be there at all. Just as Charlotte became curious about these dark patches the patches themselves moved. Charlotte was too shocked to react, and before she could regain her senses the shadows had fallen to the floor and were on her. She tried to scream but no sound came, and before she could struggle something was carrying her towards the window and into the night.

James thought he heard a noise from Charlotte's room. He was about to bang on the wall, to tell her to be quiet, when something grabbed his arm as he swung it. Confusion overtook him as he tried to work out what was holding him. It looked like a shadow but couldn't be, he must be dreaming.

James tried to sit up, but something else now pinned him down. He was lifted and taken out his bed and moved towards the window. The window was pushed open, and James was carried out into the night. He had the sensation of flying, but he was not in control. James looked to his left and saw Charlotte being carried in the same fashion by what looked like several shadows.

Confused and scared he tried to scream and struggle but could do neither. As he continued to look around him, he saw more and more children floating silently through the air, carried by these dark creatures. He realised that the direction they were taking them was back to the caves they had visited earlier.

His mind raced through some of the stories Peter's Granddad had told them through the years. Surely, they could not be true. Panic gripped him; he struggled to break free, but it was useless. The shadow walkers' work had begun, and it seemed nothing would stop them.

Up in the mansion house, George had just got comfortable in his bed when he realised he had left the window open. How annoying he thought, as he got up to shut it, he stopped in his tracks. There was a shadow sitting in the chair over by the window. Only there couldn't be because there was no one for the shadow to belong to.

Silently it rose up as another dark shape floated in through the window. Together they stepped very slowly towards George. He tried to call out but couldn't. He tried to move his legs, but they would not obey the command. The shadows were just about to reach him when a bright light filled the room, and the knight in the painting came to life. His sword glowed, and he cut through the shadows which disintegrated right in front of George. I am dreaming he thought to himself, I must be, this can't happen. The knight looked at George then moved to the window and closed it.

'Go to Peter then head for the study, the time is here.' The knight said then turned to stand guard at the window. 'Hurry they will know who we are now, and others will come. This is just the beginning.'

George finally got his legs to move and hurried next door to Peter's room where he found Peter on his bed, wide awake, staring at his window. Standing in front of the window, with his sword drawn, was the knight from Peter's painting. Outside the window a shadow creature floated silently, seemingly staring into the room. Then it was gone, and the knight turned to face the boys.

'Get to the study your Granddad will know what to do.' He said no more and turned back towards the window.

George grabbed Peter, and the boys ran down the stairs to the study followed by Jake. They opened the door stopping in their tracks. Both gryphons from the library were now alive and in the study. One was watching the window while the other was being stroked by Granddad.

'It seems I was right, and we have no time to lose,' he began, ushering the boys to sit.

'The shadow walkers are amongst us, which means children will be going missing from all over the Cove and nearby areas. They have made several attempts to get in here and soon their masters will know what this mansion is.'

'What is this mansion?' asked Peter.

'This mansion is this Cove's defence against attacks like tonight. This mansion is where we prepare to fight.'

'How can all these statues and paintings come to life?' Asked George, staring at the gryphon by the window.

'This mansion holds a powerful magic that lies dormant until an enemy tries to attack. That attack began tonight, releasing the magic.' Granddad said rising from his chair and taking a quick look out the window.

'Every statue, painting and rug in this house that holds a picture of a knight or some beast you thought was mythical is, in fact, a guardian. They will protect this house and all who are in it from any form of attack, and more of them will become active as the attacks increase.'

George was about to ask a question when there was a loud knocking on the front door. Granddad stood up and moved out to the hallway followed by the boys and one of the gryphons. The two knights at the bottom of the stairs had now come to life and were standing in a defensive position.

'Who's there?' Granddad called.

'Jacob, it's us, the attack has begun. We must act now.'

Granddad rushed to the door opening it quickly. Three men walked in and headed straight for the study. They did not seem surprised to see the gryphon or the knights and smiled at the boys as they passed them. With everyone in the study, Granddad explained who the visitors were.

'These are the church Elders. They know all about the mansion and the true history of the cove.' He turned to the Elders then continued to speak.

'Tell me what you know, what's happening out there right now?'

'Children have started to disappear, parents are scared, and the small police force cannot cope.' One of the Elders said.

'Have you done what is expected of you?' Granddad asked.

'We have, but it will not last long. We must act now. It is time to awaken all the guardians and go to the caves before it is too late.' Another added.

'We have the Longship, and we have the guardians. We are ready this time, and there is no Tolldruck to contend with.' Granddad replied.

'I'll wake all the guardians then we will go to the caves and bring the children back. George and Peter, you must remain here. I cannot put you at risk in the caves.'

'We want to come, we want to help, what if they have Charlotte and James?'

'The boys could go to the Longship. They would be safe there with the Viking guardians.' One of the Elders said.

'That's true enough; boys you must go with Elder Sanderson and stay with the Longship. I cannot take you with me to the caves; it's too dangerous. You will be safe on the ship, and you can join us later if need be.' Granddad said.

Before the boys could argue there was a loud roar from outside the study. Granddad grabbed the sword, rushing past the boys into the hall. The boys followed on after the Elders, stopping dead in their tracks as soon as they were out of the study.

The dragon from the large rug was standing at the foot of the stairs with one creature pinned under its foot while another had already been defeated and was lying broken by the front door. The two knights from the bottom of the stairs were fighting off more of the creatures who were coming from the kitchen. The gryphons gave a shrill cry and raced to the join the fight.

'Goblins!' shouted Granddad. 'They've found a way in, be careful and stay together.'

Granddad charged with a speed that defied his age, cutting down three goblins before they knew what had happened. Together the knights, gryphons and Granddad began to win the fight, pushing the goblins back into the kitchen. The old dog flap was lying broken on the floor.

The remaining goblins growled and shrieked as they were forced back and out through the flap into the night. Granddad turned around to make sure the boys were ok then asked the knights to guard the kitchen. He moved back into the hall to talk to the boys as the three knights from the picture in the games room came in. They bowed to Granddad, standing ready.

A loud cry from the top of the stairway drew everyone's attention to the giant eagle from the upstairs library and next to it the dragon from the bathroom. Beneath them both, looking slightly less imposing, was Jake who barked then ran down to join Peter.

'The guardians are all coming to life; the threat to this place is increasing.' One of the Elders said.

'Then we must act quickly and go and summon the others.' Granddad replied.

'Boys, go to the Longship and stay close to the guardians. I have a special one to look after you while I am gone.' Said Granddad turning towards his study as a large shadow fell on the doorway.

Soon the shadow filled the door then stretched into the hall. A large bear strode into the hall, even on all fours it just made it through the doorway. It looked to Granddad; they stared at each other before the bear nodded and began to move to the basement. Granddad told the boys to follow.

There was no point in protesting so Peter, George and Jake followed the bear into the basement passage. Elder Sanderson came with them, and to their amazement, he began to talk to the bear.

'It's good to see you Arto; it has been an age since we have walked side by side.'

The bear growled then nodded in agreement.

'It has been too long Elder, and I wish it were in better circumstances.' Arto replied. Peter and George exchanged stunned looks and Peter mouthed 'He talks' to George who just nodded his head staring at the bear.

'You boys will be safe with me. I owe your Granddad my life and will not let any harm come to you.' Arto turned and looked at each boy in turn.

'Wh-what do you mean you owe him your life?' George asked.

The bear was about to answer when the Elder placed his hand on the bear and shook his head.

'The boys do not know everything?' Arto asked the Elder.

'Not yet, and I think it should be for Peter's Granddad to tell them.'

Arto nodded in silent agreement and continued down the passage. Arto froze as they entered the underground harbour. The boys and the Elder stood still watching the giant bear looking from left to right scanning the whole area as the lights came on.

He walked slowly out into the middle of the stone floor and stood very still. Without any warning he dashed to the left, rising up on two legs, letting out a roar that shook the whole basement. Arto flashed out one powerful paw grabbing a shadow on the wall; the shadow started to squirm and tried to free itself. Arto ignored the struggle calmly walking over to the Elder.

'Ah a shadow walker, this will be your last night walking the darkness.' Elder Sanderson said reaching into the inside pocket of his coat, pulling out a small bottle that had a very bright, almost glowing, liquid in it.

The shadow walker screeched and struggled even harder, but it was no use Arto would not let go. The Elder unscrewed the lid and a single drop of the glowing liquid fell onto the shadow walker. Instantly the struggling stopped, and Arto let go. The creature fell to the floor without a sound or sign of life.

The light from the single drop began to spread slowly at first then picked up speed. The shadow walker was transformed into a being full of light before it shone so brightly the boys had to shield their eyes. Then as quickly as the light appeared it began to fade and with it the shadow walker faded too until there was nothing left.

'What was in that bottle?' asked George looking at the spot where the creature had been.

'Would you believe me if I said liquid sunshine?' replied the Elder smiling at George.

'Right now, I would believe anything you told me.' George replied still looking for any trace of the shadow walker.

'They do not like the daylight, and they especially do not like sunshine. It affects almost all of them, and when used correctly will kill them. There is one, which I pray we never meet who can walk in the daytime and is more powerful than all the others.' Elder Sanderson's voice showed a touch of fear, and his hand moved over a faint scar on his neck as he talked.

The Elder caught himself touching the scar and stopped, then muttered something neither boy could hear before approaching the mural of the Vikings. He ran his hand over the writing on the boat, continuing to mutter as he went. He paused and pressed his hand against part of the writing then took out another bottle from his coat.

He whispered something, placed a drop of the liquid from this new bottle onto his fingertip before circling the word he stopped at three times. He then stepped back and waited. Just as Peter was about to question what was going on the mural shuddered, and some small stones fell to the ground. A faint glow started from the word the Elder had circled, spreading to each of the Vikings in the picture.

One by one they began to move then disappear. Soon there were no Vikings left in the mural. The Elder turned his head to the Longship and smiled. The Vikings began to appear on board taking the same places they had held on the mural.

The Elder clapped his hands and moved towards the Longship.

'What word did you circle Mr Sanderson?' asked Peter

'The word in the language of the Viking is hlifa, but to you or me it means protect. It is time for the Vikings to protect their leader and their leader's descendants.' The Elder replied.

'Who is their leader, who are you talking about?' George questioned.

'All in good time, but now we must get on board and go out to the Cove and wait.'

The boys followed the Elder and Arto on to the Longship and waited while the Elder spoke with the Vikings. Jake stood next to Arto looking even smaller next to the huge bear. The large Viking at the front stood and faced the others.

'Segl, Segl,' he shouted to them.

'He is telling them to sail.' Arto said to the boys seeing the unasked question in their eyes. The Longship began to rock, and the boys were asked to sit as they set off through a dark winding underground river out into the Cove.

Back at the house Granddad and the remaining two Elders brought the other guardians together to devise their plan. The eagle and the two dragons were sent to watch the sea; they would alert anyone if ships were seen leaving. The great double doors of the mansion provided just enough room for the dragons to squeeze themselves through, and then they were gone into the night.

The gryphons and four of the knights would escort the three men as they headed for the caves. The other knights would remain behind ensuring nothing else entered the mansion.

With the plan in place, Granddad went upstairs into the spare room next to George's room. He used a large key to unlock the door and switched on the lights. Inside there were four paintings of Viking warriors and in the middle of the room a case with a helmet and shield inside.

He looked at each of the pictures in turn and uttered the words 'hofi neinn lengr minn brooir, aevi til bardagi.' Sleep no longer my brothers, time to fight.

As soon as the words were spoken the four Vikings awoke and stepped out to stand side by side with Granddad.

'The witches have returned we must hurry.' Without another word Granddad removed his helmet and shield from the case and led the other men downstairs.

As they reached the bottom of the stairs, they were met by the guardians and the Elders.

'Everyone is awake, and now we take the battle to the caves.'

'They will be expecting us, Jacob; they will be watching the entrances to all the caves.' Elder Andersen said.

'Then we will go in another way.' Granddad replied. 'Follow me.'

He turned and headed for the back door, passing two knights standing guard. He led the group out to the fountain in the back garden. Without a word the other four Vikings moved to positions around the fountain. Granddad then took his place, and all five drew their swords. Each man placed his sword in one of the rectangular holes in the base, and as they did so the water stopped running, and a deep grumbling sound began beneath their feet.

The entire fountain rose out of the ground as the men withdrew their swords and stood back. The fountain rose then moved back revealing a passageway that sloped down into darkness.

'There are torches inside that liquid sunshine will light. The Elders and I will each take one; everyone else will position themselves between the torches. The gryphons will take up the rear in case we are surprised.' Granddad explained before heading into the tunnel. One by one they stepped into the tunnel and began their descent into the caves.

Now this is interesting it thought to itself, where do they think they are going? At least now it knew for sure that Jacob was still alive and could warn the Master. It floated down to the tunnel and had to admit it admired the work that had gone into concealing the entrance.

It would give them just enough of a head start to think they were not being followed then it would send in the ogres. They should just about fit into the tunnel. It might even go itself, after all even the Shadow King needed to have some fun too.

Chapter 9

'So, Jacob has discovered our plans.' The Master said, rising from their chair to gaze out the window into the darkness where all around them their plan was taking place.

'We cannot allow him to interfere again, are the ogres ready?'

'Yes Master, they are ready and waiting for your order.' The Shadow King replied. 'If it pleases you, I would like to go as well.'

'You can lead the ogres but stay away from Jacob. He may be old, but we know how dangerous he can be.' The Master paused before going on.

'Where are the children and that terrible dog? I should have eaten him when he escaped into our garden, but I did not want to arouse suspicion or have the children poking around the house.'

'The children were not with Jacob, Master. They must still be inside the house, protected by the magic.' the Shadow King said.

'All of our goblins that went into that mansion have vanished, and with Jacob coming out I can only assume they are all dead.'

'If the children are still in there, we could use them to distract Jacob. It will be worthwhile checking.' the Master replied.

'If we send more goblins, they will die, Master. Even I would struggle to come out of there alive.'

'I was thinking of sending something a bit more useful than a goblin to search for the children.' the Master said as a wicked smile spread across her face.

'My sisters are already in the caves working with Graff and his army loading the prisoners on the ship. You go with the ogres and attack Jacob. I will join you in the caves once I have sent my friend next door to find those children.'

The Shadow King left to gather the ogres while the Master went into the back garden. She walked down to the bottom where she could see the ocean and the caves. Beneath her feet, right now, her plan was in action. She could not allow Jacob to spoil it again.

She knew she needed the children; he would do nothing if she captured them. The Master turned and raised her arms. She whispered some words then opened her mouth letting out a sound so high pitched it was above the hearing of humans. She waited patiently then she heard the return call, a loud booming roar. He was coming.

Jacob stopped suddenly in the tunnel shaking his head from side to side.

'What is it, Jacob?' asked Elder Thomson, putting his hand on Jacob's shoulder.

''I'm not sure. I felt something go right through my head, but it has passed now.' Granddad replied.

He composed himself before continuing to lead the group down towards the cave system.

*****

The boys sat on the Longship with the Elder and Arto while the Vikings rowed silently through the water out towards the Cove. The large Viking at the front of the ship raised his hand and slowly they stopped.

'Why are we stopping?' Peter asked with Jake fast asleep on his lap.

'We must wait here for a signal from either the watchers in the sky or from your Granddad then we will know what action to take.'

'Who is my Granddad?' Peter asked. 'I mean I know he's my Granddad but who is he really?'

'Your Granddad is a great man who has done a lot for the Cove, and for people in general. His work had kept people safe when most of the time they never knew they were in danger.' Arto replied.

'The time will come when he will tell you the whole story of his life, but it is for him to tell. Your Granddad would be hurt if anyone else did the telling for him.' Elder Sanderson said watching Peter and George.

'It is all just so much to take in, why did he not tell us any of this before? Why has he not told my mum?'

'What could he have said? Could he have told your parents he was concerned that witches were going to attack his home?' Arto said looking at the boys. 'Should he have said he has a friend who is a talking bear that can vouch for his story?' Arto seemed to smile as he said this.

'No, you are right. I know you are. It's just so much to deal with.' Peter looked to George hoping he would back him up.

'I am on a Longship with a talking bear and Vikings that came out of a painting. I have seen shadows come alive and try to steal me. I have watched goblins fight knights and gryphons in a house! I think it's safe to say your Granddad is more than you thought he was, that's for sure.' He looked out over the dark sea before continuing.

'This is also, without a doubt, the strangest start to a summer ever.' George said, punching Peter in the arm, and letting out a small laugh. Peter laughed as well. He was glad his friend was with him.

*****

As the boys waited on the Longship Granddad and his companions continued through the tunnel. They moved silently not wanting to attract any unwanted attention. They were making good progress, and Granddad thought they would be in the caves within a few minutes. Suddenly one of the gryphons let out a shrill cry, and the group stopped. Granddad and the other Vikings moved back past the others to see what had alarmed the gryphon. Now both gryphons turned to face the darkness growling nervously.

'What is it? What do you see?' Granddad asked peering into the darkness. He moved his torch through the air but could see nothing. The gryphons continued to stare into the darkness, their hearing and sense of smell both acuter than that of the men. The fact that they were anxious was reason enough for Granddad to feel uneasy.

'Draw your swords and stay close to the light, do not wander from the group.' Granddad said drawing his weapon slowly, never taking his eyes off the darkness behind them.

'What is it, Jacob?' asked one of the Vikings, drawing his sword.

'I am not sure, but whatever it is it has scared the gryphons, and that is all the warning we need. We are not alone in this tunnel anymore.'

The tunnel began to shake, slowly at first, just little bits of soil moving across the ground, then the noise came. Quiet to begin with, the sound of something approaching far away, but quickly closing the distance to the group. Still, they could see nothing. More and more dirt fell from the ceiling tumbling across the floor.

The group stood ready in the narrow tunnel. A fight here would not be easy, but the alternative was to turn their back on whatever this danger was. The sound of heavy feet pounding the soft tunnel floor echoed all around, accompanied by frenzied shrieks and growls. The enemy was close now, but still, they could see nothing.

The Shadow King led the ogres down the tunnel hiding them in his darkness. He would pull back when they were almost upon their prey, hoping the element of surprise would give the ogres the edge. He could see the light cast by their torches. He had no doubt they were using liquid sunshine, and he would have to be careful.

The ogres were in full charge now, full of blood lust and ready for a fight. They turned a sloping corner in the tunnel and there seconds from them was Jacob, his sword drawn, with the two gryphons by his side. The Shadow King waited until the very last second before withdrawing his darkness and revealing the ogres. The ogres shrieked in delight when they saw their enemy, raising their short swords, daggers and clubs to attack.

'Ogres!' Granddad cried as suddenly the tunnel was full of the foul beasts charging down on them.

The gryphons were the first of the group to move, thrusting forward powerfully knocking over the nearest ogres before they could react. Granddad and the Vikings charged meeting the ogres head on, swords clashed, shields smashed off clubs and noise filled the tunnel.

Ogres were being slain quickly as the Vikings moved with amazing speed cutting through them. They were helped by the gryphons while the knights guarded the Elders. As more and more ogres fell, more and more came, there seemed to be no end to their charge. The tunnel was filling with their lifeless bodies as Granddad and the Vikings continued their attack.

Granddad realised they were getting further away from the Elders; he called for them to hold then slowly retreat to their companions. They continued to fight off the ogres as they backed up. The ogres were less enthusiastic for the battle as they stepped over the bodies of so many of their kind to get to their enemies.

The Shadow King could see the ogres were being routed by the Vikings, but he also saw an opportunity to inflict some revenge. Unseen as the battle raged below him, he rose to the tunnel roof and crept past the fight, hovering above the knights guarding the Elders.

The Shadow King dropped in front of them just as the Vikings began to move back in their direction. He reached out for one of the knights pulling him into the suffocating darkness. The other knights reacted far quicker than the Shadow King thought they would, and a strike caught the King on his neck.

The blow would have killed a Shadow Walker but merely forced the King backwards. He regained his composure and crushed the final breaths of life out of the knight he gripped in his darkness. The knight's body fell to the ground as the King moved towards the others, twisting his form, changing the darkness to confuse them.

They struck out wildly with their swords every stroke missing. He attacked again in one swift movement, lifting another knight into his darkness then throwing him effortlessly against the wall. He turned to face the remaining two knights, swirling his darkness into an ever-changing flow of shapes making it impossible for them to attack.

He was having fun now and swooped in pulling away their swords, dropping them out of reach. He gave them a glimpse of his face, dark red eyes and razor-sharp teeth, before disappearing into his darkness for another attack.

Pain shot across him, he swirled and turned to see Jacob swiping at him with his liquid sunshine torch. It burned as pain ripped through his body. The Shadow King screamed and fled down the tunnel towards the caves. He cursed Jacob and vowed there would be another meeting.

Jacob checked on the two fallen knights, both were dead, the only casualties of the battle. Tens of ogres lay stricken, and others had retreated up the tunnel, deserted by their leader, with the battle lost.

'We must go now and make for the caves as quickly as we can. The Shadow King will alert them that we are coming. They will be waiting for us.'

Jacob turned to the gryphons and continued.

'I must ask one of you to go back up the tunnel and tell the others they to prepare to join the fight. We have lost the element of surprise.'

One of the gryphons bowed its head before racing off up the tunnel. The remaining ogres would already be out the tunnel, and either hiding or making their way down to the caves. Jacob cast his light over the scene of the battle; broken ogre bodies lay everywhere. He took one last regretful look at the bodies of the knights then led the others on towards the caves.

*****

Back at the house, the knights continued to guard the kitchen where the goblins had come in. There had been no repeat attacks, and it appeared that the enemy had moved on. Still, the knights stayed at their post protecting the mansion. A roar shattered the silence and the ground shook.

The sound of heavy footsteps smashed into the ground. The roar came again, and they prepared for whatever was coming. Pots and dishes fell to the ground, smashing all over the kitchen floor. They drew their swords stepping backwards in unison ready to fight.

Tolldruck burst through the kitchen wall splintering the door into a hundred pieces sending brick and glass in every direction. He spotted the knights straight away and raced for them using his powerful forearms to deflect their blows, before smashing them aside with ease. He was here for the children and could not concern himself with the knights.

He broke open doors searching rooms for any signs of them but could not find them anywhere. He roared as he raced upstairs in two bounds his large body barely fitting on the hallway. He checked every room without finding what he was looking for. He left a trail of destruction behind him, partly meant partly unavoidable due to his size.

He leapt back to the hall in one movement, crashing into the floor by the stairs, perfectly balanced, as one of the knights was regaining consciousness. Tolldruck grabbed him, lifting him off the ground as if he was a feather. He peered at the knight opening his mouth to reveal the rows of razor-sharp teeth; his forked tongue darted in and out.

'Where are the children?' He growled crushing the knight in his grip. The knight said nothing and stared back at the beast defiantly.

'You cannot save them, but you can save yourself.' Tolldruck said loosening his grip slightly to give the knight a chance to talk.

The knight raised a hand and nodded his head as if he were about to talk. Tolldruck released him and as he fell to the floor, the knight produced a dagger from under his armour and made a desperate attempt to stab Tolldruck. The blade did not penetrate his tough black skin. Tolldruck disarmed the knight and threw him full force into the wall under the stairs. His shattered body struck the secret switch revealing the basement passageway. Tolldruck smiled to himself and roared before running into the basement.

Chapter 10

They reached the cave system as quickly as possible, slowing down only when they could see the lights and hear the sounds of the commotion below them on the cavern floor. Granddad crept forward and looked over a rocky ledge; the scene was familiar and frightening at the same time.

Goblins and trolls herded scared children into cages that were then lifted by ogres into the hold of a large ship. The children were crying and screaming while the monsters mocked and taunted them. A group stood watching the activity having a heated conversation.

Granddad could not hear what was being said, but he recognised the three sisters from the house next door. The one that brought Jake back appeared to be leading the talk and was very animated. She struck out sending a troll flying across the cavern, eventually landing twenty feet from the group.

Granddad watched as the Shadow King appeared and talked directly to the sister. They both looked up to where the group were hiding. The sister began to shout, and soon trolls and goblins were heading up the winding path towards them.

Graff struck the floor hard after being thrown by the Master. He cursed her under his breath as blood flowed from impact wounds on his legs. Struggling to his feet, he regretted telling the Master that her sisters had done nothing but get in the way and hinder his progress.

He froze when he saw the Shadow King; only Tolldruck scared him more. Graff finally got his legs to move hurrying back to the group to grovel an apology to the Master and to find out what the King wanted.

'Spare me your apologies Graff we have more pressing matters to deal with. Jacob is here, and he has brought some old friends with him.'

'They routed the ogres, and I was lucky to escape with just a scratch.' the Shadow King hissed. 'They will be close by now, coming from above us. We must send some goblins and trolls to slow them down.'

'Graff, take some of your soldiers and workers and stop Jacob. Do not fail me or you will answer to Tolldruck.' The Master's voice was cold and distant, and her eyes turned black as she spoke.

Jacob hurried back to the group telling them what he had seen. They all stood to look down the path and could see hordes of goblins and trolls running up it in a chaotic herd. They must have outnumbered the small group twenty to one, but there was no thought of escaping back up the tunnel.

The gryphon spread its wings and rose up above the group ready to attack. The Vikings and knights drew their weapons while the Elders moved to the back.

Elder Andersen took out a small potion bottle and another small container from his pockets. He mixed both of them up then stood ready to throw the mixture. Elder Thomson smiled before doing the same.

'We can't fight like they do, but we can still make a nuisance of ourselves.' Elder Andersen said with a smile.

As the goblins and trolls approached screeching, squealing and growling, clawing at each other to get to the group, the Elders both threw their potions over the others into the first lines of the enemy. A blinding light then a furious explosion and thirty of the creatures lay dead, stopping the others in their tracks. Their noises now the whimpers of fear and uncertainty.

Seeing so many killed so quickly had removed their appetite for the fight. Graff knew he could not fail though and screamed orders at the goblins and trolls to attack. He kicked the nearest ones to him and shouted threats about Tolldruck. It was this last threat that spurred his army on. They surged forward once more drawing their crude daggers and axes ready to kill Jacob and his companions.

The gryphon struck first, swooping down and picking up four of the attackers, lifting them effortlessly into the air before dropping them to the cavern floor. The Vikings moved in led by Jacob who slashed and moved so fast the goblins and trolls were left striking at thin air before they were cut down.

Graff screamed with rage as he could see the battle was being lost, and his army seemed unable to inflict even the smallest wound on their enemy. As before the two knights stayed back and guarded the Elders, the odd goblin or troll that got past the Vikings unharmed was soon cut down by them. Jacob's sword moved with such speed and accuracy he was unstoppable. Goblins and trolls fell at his feet, some before they knew they had died.

Panic spread through Graff, not only were they losing but soon the Vikings would be upon him, and he would be required to fight, and most likely die. Graff liked to fight, but usually only when he was sure he would win. He looked around for a miracle and seeing none he moved further back while barking orders to his army.

The Master watched the scene unfolding above her, shaking her head at the ineptitude of trolls and goblins. She expected that they would lose, but she at least thought they could hold back a handful of Vikings for a while longer than it seemed they were capable of doing.

The cavern floor was littered with their broken bodies that the gryphon was dropping, and she imagined the pathway was running green with their blood. If only Tolldruck were here to stop them, but he was searching for the children. She could get involved herself but would rather that was the last resort.

She would be needed on the ship and could not risk a fight until it was out at sea. Her sisters could prove useful, but not yet. She had another plan to slow them down; a plan that made her smile.

The Master concentrated on all the dead bodies of goblins and trolls that lay around her and began casting a spell. She pointed her finger at body after body saying the spell over and over. She looked up to the pathway and said the spell again. Dead bodies of goblins and trolls began to float down to the cavern and lie with the others.

The numbers of enemies were dwindling, Jacob and the Vikings were minutes away from securing the path and getting down to the cavern floor when the bodies started to float all around them. Such was the surprise that one of the Vikings dropped his sword and immediately two of the goblins left living jumped on him striking him with their crude daggers.

He threw one against the wall while another Viking brought his axe down on the other with great accuracy and speed, stopping just as the blade cut all the way through the goblin and touched his brother's armour. After a quick inspection, a few scratches were his only injuries.

The bodies of the two slain goblins began to float like the others and move towards the cavern floor. Soon there was a large pile of bodies altogether. The group watched in astonishment as the pile began to melt, and the bodies all became one big puddle of greenish brown.

The goblins and trolls that were still alive turned and ran back down the path, led by Graff who knew what was coming and did not want to be anywhere near when it happened.

The puddle began to bubble and expand. Shapes formed then disappeared over and over. Hissing sounds turned into tortured screams and shouts. A hundred voices could be heard all at once, then suddenly everything stopped, and the puddle became still.

'I don't like this, Jacob.' Elder Andersen said.

'Neither do I; I have a terrible feeling about this.' Jacob replied not taking his eyes off the puddle.

The puddle began to move again although this time there seemed to be some order to the movements. First, an eye appeared then another, they blinked and looked around as if they were aware of their surroundings. One eye was yellow with a red pupil and the other was red with a yellow pupil.

A head began to take shape around the eyes and rise out of the puddle. A hooked nose formed and below it a snarling ugly mouth full of row after row of large, ragged teeth. A jet-black tongue, the size of a python, darted in and out.

The group watched the transformation terrified.

'It's a Goliath.' Jacob shouted to the others.

The huge monster rose up as more of the body formed. Large, powerful arms with the muscles of trolls and the razor-sharp claws of goblins grew out of the dark green body. The head snapped round until it fixed eyes with the Master who communicated some hidden message without uttering a sound.

The beast turned to face the pathway and roared. It looked down at itself seemingly anxious for the legs to form so it could do what it had been created for. Finally, it was complete, standing twenty feet tall, powerful and confident. It flexed both arms, stretched out the clawed fingers and stamped the huge feet.

Intelligent eyes took in the pathway, and the group as it weighed up the options for attack. It knew no fear and had the combined speed and strength of every troll and goblin that had been used to create it. One leap and it was on the pathway facing the group who formed a battle formation while the gryphon took flight ready to attack. The Elders made another couple of potions, and a tense standoff began as they sized each other up.

The Master was happy with her creation. The Goliath should keep them busy, and if she was lucky, it might kill them all and save her the trouble. She searched for Graff and found him hiding in a dark corner. She pointed at him, and he was forced to her, flying through the air into her iron grip.

'Can you do nothing right?' she asked. 'Why do I keep you alive Graff?' The questions did not require to be answered which was just as well as Graff could barely breath never mind speak.

'Go and make sure everything is secure, we are leaving right now.' She let go of Graff and with a wave of her hand he was thrown towards the ship.

*****

In the Longship the boys waited for what seemed like an age. Jake barely stirred, happy on Peter's lap. No one on board spoke, and there was a tension in the air. Arto looked towards the caves waiting and hoping for a signal. The gryphon's cry was faint at first growing louder each time.

The cry was answered by the eagle that swooped down to fly side by side with the gryphon. They spoke to each other in a series of squawks and cries then the eagle turned towards the caves and was gone. The gryphon continued towards the Longship landing next to Arto. Straight away the gryphon began to squawk and Arto listened, nodding then asking questions.

Arto turned to the Vikings. 'We sail for the caves now!' he commanded in a booming roar. The Vikings needed no further encouragement, and the Longship began to sail for the caves.

'What's wrong?' Peter asked standing up, sending Jake to the deck. Jake gave a disapproving bark in Peter's direction before resting against George's leg.

'Your Granddad has been discovered in the caves, and they need our help.' Arto replied.

'It's time to join the fight.'

*****

Tolldruck ran into the underground harbour taking in his surroundings. He sniffed the air and moved instantly to the spot where the Shadow Walker had been killed. He growled then walked over to the picture, one clawed hand circled where the Elder had touched. He walked to the edge of the water, breathed in deeply before roaring and diving in. He could sense his prey was close.

*****

Elder Thomson's nerve broke first; he threw his potion at the Goliath. The explosion was as ferocious and bright as before. The Goliath was sent backwards crashing into the wall; stones fell over him as he struggled to regain his senses. The Goliath shook his head from side to side brushing off the effects of the blast. The few cuts the explosion had caused were already healing.

Before the Goliath had completely recovered Elder Andersen sent his potion into the wall above the beast burying him under a large pile of stones and rocks.

The Elders cheered, patting each other on the back, and Elder Thomson clenched his fist in celebration. The Vikings were not so quick to claim victory. They stayed in formation watching the rubble pile. The Goliath burst from the pile, roaring, but still did not attack.

'Why does it not attack?' Asked one of the Vikings. Jacob looked to the cavern floor then back to the Goliath.

'He's trying to give them time to escape.' He said pointing to the activity below. 'We must not allow them that luxury.' Jacob spoke louder so all the group could hear him. 'To hurt a Goliath, you have to sever limbs. They will grow back but at least we can slow him down long enough to get past him.' With that, he raised his sword and charged.

The sword changed colour and glowed orange as Jacob swung to try and sever a hand. The Goliath moved with surprising speed, only losing a couple of fingers before slamming Jacob into the ground with its other hand.

The Vikings moved in as one, slashing and cutting at the beast which feinted then sent two Vikings into the wall with one swing of its left arm. The gryphon swooped, raking his talons across the Goliath's face, retreating before being hit.

Jacob was back on his feet moving unnoticed as the Goliath concentrated on the Vikings. He brought his sword across the Achilles of the right foot severing the foot completely. The roar of pain was instant as the Goliath stumbled and fell off the pathway crashing onto the cavern floor.

'Run! We must get down to the cavern before the Goliath has healed.'

The group gathered the injured Vikings and ran as fast as possible down the pathway towards the ship with the gryphon flying overhead. The Goliath was hurt but not defeated. The foot was growing, back and the broken bones it suffered in the fall were already healing.

The Master watched on, with her sisters, aboard the ship almost ready to sail. She smiled as the Goliath got to his feet roaring with rage before running towards the group.

'Set sail Graff; we must get to sea before they are passed the Goliath.'

Graff ran to the front of the ship and blew the large horn. Two gigantic creatures raised out of the water each holding a rope in their mouth. The ropes were attached to the front of the ship. The creatures began to swim out to sea taking the ship and the prisoners with them.

The Master raised her hands as the ship began to move and slowly recited some ancient magic. Sparks appeared from her fingers and danced all around her. Soon the sparks from her were flowing over the ship.

Her sisters joined in and within seconds the eggshell along the bottom of the ship began to glow, and the water around them bubbled. Outside of the caves clouds filled the sky, and thunder began to rumble. A large flash of lightning cut across the sky just as their ship left the caves. The Master smiled. She was confident nothing would stop them now.

The group rounded the last corner just as the Goliath charged, it was not holding back any longer. The Vikings met the charge, dodging and slashing again and again. A mistake by one gave the Goliath the chance it was waiting for, and it smashed one strong arm into his body sending him flying through the air, crashing against the wall then slumping to the ground.

The gryphon swooped, though this time, the Goliath was ready, ducking out the way then swinging through one powerful turn, grabbing the gryphon in mid-flight. There was no time to react as the Goliath crushed the gryphon, dropping it lifeless to the ground.

'No!' Jacob yelled, filling with anger as he charged, ducking under one giant clawed hand. He spun round bringing his sword down cutting off the hand at the wrist. Before the Goliath could recover Jacob struck again taking off half of its' left foot. The Vikings and knights joined in, attacking the Goliath from all sides.

One arm was chopped off above the elbow, and the right leg was severed at the knee forcing the beast to collapse. Jacob rushed in standing by the head, and with one mighty swing took it clean off.

Jacob ran over to the gryphon, but it was too late; tears filled his eyes as he watched the Elders check the fallen Viking. Elder Thomson rose, looking at Jacob, shaking his head. He turned to look at the Goliath and despaired to see it reforming once again. The beast was almost entirely regrown.

He wondered how they could ever kill this monster when a loud roar came from where the ship had been a few moments before. The dragons swooped in, blasting fire at the Goliath, landing between it and Jacob. They circled the Goliath as the attack continued relentlessly.

Fire with ferocious heat and intensity shot from their mouths blast after blast. The Goliath stumbled and curled up into a ball trying to protect itself from the attack. The fire kept coming, turning the Goliath to nothing more than a pile of smouldering ash. The remaining gryphon and the eagle arrived landing next to Jacob.

'You did well my friend.' Jacob said to the gryphon stroking its back. The gryphon left Jacob's side, going over to the body of the other gryphon nudging it with its nose. It licked the face of the dead gryphon as a low sound of pain and sorrow came from it.

'I'm sorry, he fought well and was very brave.' Jacob said. 'We must go now if we are to have any chance of catching the ship.'

The gryphon looked up to the cavern roof letting out the loudest cry it could. It was almost the sound of a scream, haunting and pained.

'We are too far behind. How will we get to the Longship in time?' asked Elder Andersen.

'We fly.' Jacob replied pointing at the dragons and the eagle. They seemed to understand and lay as flat as they could on the cavern floor. The Vikings and the Elders got on the two dragons while the two knights got on the eagle. Jacob got on the gryphon.

'Hold on tight.' Jacob said to the others as the gryphon took to the air, leading them out to sea.

Chapter 11

The boys watched as the large ship crashed out on to the waves and began to sail out to sea. Oars appeared and soon the ship was moving quickly away from the Cove. There was lots of activity on board, and creatures of all shapes and sizes could be seen walking around. Two enormous beasts at the front seemed to be guiding the ship. As the oars came out and the ship moved to deeper waters, the giant beasts dived, and were gone.

'Where's Granddad?' Peter asked Elder Sanderson.

'He must still be in the caves, which means the witches have escaped.' Elder Sanderson replied looking at Arto, who turned and went to speak to the leader of the Vikings.

'We must follow the ship and trust that Jacob will find us before it is too late.' The Elder continued. 'We cannot allow those children to be taken without a fight.'

'Our friends are probably on that ship.' George said, staring out at the ship in the distance.

A roar overhead made them all look up as the dragons and the eagle sped into the caves.

'They are going to help your Granddad.' Arto said returning from his talk with the Viking. 'Don't worry your Granddad will be with us soon enough. The Vikings are agreed that we must keep chasing the witch ship. We cannot allow them to get back to their world.'

'We can't let them take Charlotte and James, we just can't.' Peter said.

Just then shapes emerged from the cave flying fast, heading straight for the Longship. The gryphon let out a cry to let them know it was friends who approached. The gryphon landed on the boat, and Granddad got off and spoke to the gryphon before turning to face the boys.

Peter ran across and hugged him close. Jake barked and bounced around trying to join in. Granddad reached down to stroke his head. George smiled at the reunion and his relief that Granddad was ok. The dragons were too large to land on the Longship so got as close as they could before the Vikings and Elders jumped off. The eagle landed near the boys, and the knights got off joining the others.

Granddad filled everyone in on what had happened in the caves including the sad news of the death of the Viking and the gryphon.

'We must ensure their death is not in vain, we have to stop that ship.' Granddad said, looking at each of the group in turn until his eyes met Peter's.

'This Longship is faster than their ship even in the storms that their magic will cause, and we will catch up to them before too long. When we do, we must be ready to fight, and save those children.' He paused then continued.

'For now, though I need to speak to Peter alone. There are a great many things I have to try and explain, and not much time to explain them.'

Everyone moved away apart from George who was reluctant to leave.

'Granddad I would like George to stay too, he deserves to hear everything you have to say.'

Granddad looked at George then back to Peter and nodded. George moved up so that he was sitting right next to Peter, facing Granddad.

'Where to start, that is always the hardest part.' Granddad said almost to himself, stroking Jake, staring at the ground.

'Some of what I am about to say you may find hard to believe, but maybe not so hard with everything you have seen tonight. Still, it is only fair to warn you.'

'I don't think you could shock us any more than we are already.' Peter replied.

'The first thing is always the hardest to explain or to say so I am just going to say it. Please don't ask any questions until I am finished as time is short.' The boys nodded in silent agreement.

'Good. I find just saying it is the easiest way so I will. My name is Jacob Thorsten, and I am Viking. I am over five hundred years old and was at one point immortal. I am the Viking warrior who fought the dragons, and I am the Viking who has battled these witches before. I am the one who faced Tolldruck, and I am also the warrior who gave up their prize for love. For the love of your Gran to be precise.' Granddad paused and stared at the boys who were looking at him wide-eyed and speechless.

'This Longship is mine and has been with me since I arrived here to rid the Cove of dragons. The sail that you brought me was passed down through my family for centuries and was with your mother to keep safe until I needed it again.'

'There is a deep magic within my mansion; a magic which, with the help of the Elders, has been perfected over many years and through many failures. This magic allows us to call upon our friends and the guardians to join us and fight side by side when the evil returns.'

'I suspected the witches may be back and started making plans and getting organised. I had thought about cancelling your holiday but then your mother would have come to the Cove and placed herself in danger.'

'What about me? Did you not worry about me being in danger?' Peter asked looking slightly hurt.

'Of course I did Peter. However, your story and your legacy are just beginning.'

'Legacy, what do you mean legacy?'

'You are my first male descendant, there are things about yourself that you do not even realise yet.' Granddad continued.

'It was always my intention to tell you everything one day. To train you so that you could take my place to guard against the evil that threatens this world.'

'Me? You mean me? There is nothing special about me. I can't use a sword the way I watched you doing. I can't lead Vikings and gryphons or use magic.'

'You can do a great many things you are unaware of just now, and it's my job to train you.'

'What about me?' George asked. 'I want to help as well, and I want to get our friends back then make sure these witches never return.'

'You are finding bravery George, and I suspect you will always have a role by Peter's side, but it is Peter who is my heir.'

'We can talk more about this when we have rescued all the children and banished the witches. For now, though we need to take care. There is a storm coming.' Granddad said, pointing into the distance where the witches' ship was closer now and was surrounded by dark clouds as lightning cracked across the sky.

'I must talk to the others. Stay safe boys and stay near Arto or me at all times.' With that Granddad stood up and walked across to the Elders. He said something to Arto who nodded and came to stand close to the boys.

'You know what this makes you, don't you Peter?' asked George.

'No, what?' replied Peter.

'The Viking's Apprentice.' George said, staring out to the storm.

Chapter 12

Granddad spoke to the others, discussing their plan of attack once they had caught up to the witches' ship.

'We must stop them before they get back to the portal and return to their world. The gryphon has gone on ahead to find the portal, so we will know how much time we have.'

Elder Andersen was about to speak when something hit the bottom of the ship. The Vikings talked to each other in raised voices, moving to all sides of the ship to see what they had hit.

'It can't be rocks we are too far out now.' Elder Thomson said.

A large thump and again the ship rocked in the water. The boys joined Granddad staring into the dark, choppy swollen waters below them. Jake let out a small, worried growl.

'What is it Granddad?' asked Peter.

'I have no idea Peter, the Elder is right, though. We are too far out to be hitting rocks.'

Again, the Longship rocked with an impact, then another, then another and another. Jake began to bark as panic spread through the Vikings, swords were drawn, and orders shouted. Then the rocking stopped. Whatever it was that had hit the bottom of the ship appeared to have gone. They all looked over the sides of the Longship but could see nothing.

The Vikings smiled to each other, visibly relaxing, putting away their swords and returning to their posts. Granddad did not share their change in mood, and his sword stayed drawn.

'Relax Jacob, something must have lodged under the ship, and the current caused it to knock into us until it was free.' Elder Sanderson said.

'I am not so sure.' Granddad replied.

No sooner were the words out of his mouth when something crashed into the side of the ship with enough force to throw them off their feet. Only Arto and Granddad remained unmoved as the others scrambled back to their feet. They stood silently, swords drawn once again, preparing to defend themselves. A flash of movement from the water and two Vikings disappeared over the side, lost forever, swallowed by the sea.

'What was it?' Granddad cried. 'Did anyone see what attacked?'

No one had seen the attacker, and no one wanted to take their eyes off the sea in case they were next. A flash of lightning from the storm distracted some of the Vikings who had put down their oars and drawn their swords. A roar, and a blur of movement and the swords remained but the Vikings were gone. Peter turned to his Granddad and could see a confused and scared expression on his face as the rain began to fall heavily.

'What did you see?' Peter yelled above the rain and wind.

'Stay away from the edge of the ship, get into the centre and form a circle.' Granddad yelled ignoring Peter's question.

Granddad spoke to Arto and the three remaining Vikings from the caves, who took positions outside the circle. The boys, Jake and the Elders, were placed inside the circle with the two knights guarding them. The rain lashed down hard soaking them all to the skin.

'Whatever happens, Peter do not leave the circle, whatever you hear or whatever you see, stay in the protection of the circle.' Granddad said before taking his position outside the circle next to Arto.

Two large clawed hands appeared over the bow. A low growl could be heard above the noise of the storm as Tolldruck's enormous black frame landed on the ship. The Longship tilted slightly with the weight of Tolldruck. His red eyes with their yellow pupils appeared to glow as his black forked tongue flicked in and out of his mouth. He looked at Granddad and then swung his tail around showing he had not forgotten who had taken half of it.

'Do you want me to take the other half?' Granddad shouted above the storm, giving Tolldruck a good look at the sword which had inflicted the damage.

Tolldruck smiled never taking his eyes off Granddad. Huge, frightening teeth appeared as his smile grew into a snarl. A crack of lightning lit up the ship as Tolldruck began to slowly advance towards the group. He showed no fear or concern at being hopelessly outnumbered. This was the battle, and this is what Tolldruck was born to do.

Two Vikings charged, one with a sword, and the other with an axe. Tolldruck moved faster than either and caught them both at the same time, powerful arms knocking them off their feet before they could swing their weapons. He roared turning to face the next charge. Three Vikings, this time, ran straight for him, he spun and caught one with his tail and another with a double hit from two of his powerful arms.

The third kept low and used the wet deck to slide past dangerous claws to land a blow with his axe on Tolldruck's left leg. He roared and brought his foot down hard on the Viking's arm, breaking it instantly as the axe fell to the ground. Tolldruck picked up the Viking giving him a very close look at his sharp teeth.

He was about to take a bite when a searing pain shot through one of his webbed feet. He dropped the Viking as Granddad brought his sword down again, this time slashing across the back of Tolldruck's right knee forcing him to buckle and fall. Tolldruck struck out sending Granddad flying back towards the circle.

Peter could hear his cry of pain, but the knights would not let him or Jake leave. Arto saw his chance and charged at Tolldruck smashing his full weight into him sending him back against the side of the ship. He rose up on two legs and hit Tolldruck over and over again, with his claws slashing and cutting the beast's skin.

Tolldruck managed to get to his feet, uneasy on his damaged leg, fending off the blows with his four arms. He regained his composure; the next strike from Arto was caught in a vice like grip. Tolldruck smiled as he picked up Arto in all four arms turning to throw him overboard. His knee gave way again, the damage inflicted by Granddad was too great.

Arto fell onto the deck of the ship as four Vikings charged, sensing the chance to finish Tolldruck once and for all. Injured but not defeated, Tolldruck met the charge head on using his arms as shields to deflect their swords. Minor cuts and grazes were all that their weapons could inflict on him.

He took the sword from one and thrust it through the chest of another. He roared as he sent another Viking over the side of the ship into the unforgiving sea. The fourth he sent flying with a powerful hit to the chest leaving the Viking lifeless on the floor.

His knee was badly injured. He knew he could not end this now. With a roar of defiance and anger, Tolldruck stood up and launched himself into the water, vanishing beneath the surface.

Peter ran to Granddad once it was clear the danger had passed. Granddad was getting himself unsteadily to his feet helped by two Vikings. Peter hugged him and Granddad smiled at him trying to reassure him. Jake barked and wagged his tail.

'I am ok Peter just a little bruised; it has been a while. I forgot just how strong Tolldruck was. We have not seen the last of him, but for now, we must check the others and catch up with that ship.'

Arto was back up limping heavily, but otherwise ok. Three of the Vikings on the ship were dead, and others were lost overboard. There was minor damage to the Longship but nothing that would prevent it chasing the witches' ship. Granddad, Peter and George looked over the bow towards the witches' vessel as the distance between the two began to close once again.

'The final chase begins Peter; we end this now.' Granddad said.

Chapter 13

Onboard the witches' ship the children were being kept at the bottom in cages laid out in two rows that faced each other. There was an awful smell, and it was dark and damp. Charlotte and James huddled together in a small, cramped cage with eight other children.

Now and then a troll or goblin would patrol up and down hitting the cages, laughing as the children cried and screamed. The shadow walkers who had stolen them were never far. Occasionally a dark spot on the wall would move or float away.

Charlotte was terrified, she didn't understand what had happened, and had not seen Peter or George since they had been taken. She hoped they had escaped and hoped help was on its way.

A large troll entered; bigger than the others she had seen. He was accompanied by a tall woman who Charlotte recognised as one of the sisters from next door to Peter's Granddad's house. She nudged James and pointed as the woman approached. Confusion spread over his face as he realised where he had seen her before.

The woman and the troll walked past every cage, looking in then moving on until they came to the one with Charlotte and James. The lady looked at each child in turn until her eyes rested on Charlotte.

'Finally, we have found them, Graff open this cage and take those two upstairs.' The lady said pointing a bony finger at Charlotte and James.

Graff opened the cage, and the children cowered away to the corners trying to avoid being touched by his horrible hands. He grabbed hold of Charlotte and James and pulled them through the door, dropping them on the floor in front of the woman. James had a large drop of greenish-brown slime from a burst spot on Graff's hand on his pyjama top.

'Do you know who I am?' she asked bending down to stare in their faces.

'You're Ms Kirke, and you live next door to Peter's Granddad.' Charlotte replied in a quiet, shaky voice.

'That is partly right I suppose, although there is so much more to me. I am the Master, and you are now my slaves. There is a new world waiting for you, but for now, I need you up on deck to help me with something.'

'Graff take them up to the deck and put them in the usual place for our guests.' She said with a smile.

Just then the darkness behind the Master changed and the Shadow King appeared. Charlotte screamed and James jumped back stumbling into Graff who lost his balance and fell over.

'Master, Tolldruck has arrived, and he is injured. He says the children are with Jacob and a small army of

Vikings; Arto is with them. They are catching us fast on a Longship, and we don't have much time to prepare.'

'Arto, well well, it has been a long time since I have seen him.' The Master said.

'I will speak to Tolldruck myself and ready my sisters for Jacob and his army.' She said the word army with a sneer as if she doubted such a small group could cause them any problems. She turned to Charlotte, winked, then vanished.

Graff pushed Charlotte and James through a door that took them out into a wild storm. The rain lashed down, and the wind howled as the sea swelled all around them. Oddly, there was not a drop of rain on the ship, and the wind didn't seem to have any effect onboard.

Graff guided them to two small cages on the centre of the deck and shoved them roughly inside locking the doors with chains. He smiled as pus ran from his lips down over his chin.

'I hope you're comfortable.' He said laughing as he walked away.

'Look over there.' James said, his voice trembling with fear. Charlotte looked where James was pointing and froze. A large black monster was talking to the Master. Charlotte fought the need to scream and looked away.

'What's going on?' James asked his voice breaking, and tears streaming down his cheeks. 'That Shadow thing mentioned the children were with Jacob. Do you think he meant Peter and George?'

'I don't know James. I don't understand any of this. Do you think Peter's Granddad's stories might be true?'

'What? I, eh, I-I don't know.'

'Oh, the stories are true.' The Shadow King said, appearing from nowhere, his darkness swirling around the cages.

'Especially the ones about missing children.' His red eyes flashed from within the darkness as James screamed and Charlotte fainted.

*****

The Longship was closing fast, even with the storm was battering them. Large swells lifted the ship out the water, dumping it back into the sea with tremendous force, but still the Vikings held their course, closing in on the witches' vessel. Peter and George gripped onto one of the benches as they carried on with incredible speed.

Granddad and the Vikings seemed to have no problem walking around in the storm. The only other people that were having problems were the Elders. They were also huddled together, struggling to stay upright.

'You will find your sea legs soon enough boys.' Granddad said coming to sit with them.

'Very soon we will catch up to the witches and board their ship. We have to assume they know we are coming and will be ready for us.' He paused, looking at each boy in turn, before continuing.

'It is up to both of you to decide for yourself whether or not you want to go on board their ship, and if you want to stay here that is fine.'

'I want to come. James and Charlotte might be on there, and we need to help them.' Said Peter surprising himself with how quickly he volunteered.

'Well if he's going so am I.' said George, pushing his soaking wet hair out of his eyes. 'We'll need a weapon, though.'

'Indeed, you will; Elder Thomson has just the thing.'

The Elder appeared holding what looked like water pistols full of a glowing liquid.

'This is liquid sunshine, even a small drop on the body of a troll or goblin will kill it instantly. Be very careful with it and remember just a small amount will do a lot of damage.' With that, he handed one of the pistols to each of the boys and left them with Granddad.

'We have a plan of how we are going to attack their ship and now that you have agreed to join us you must play your part.' Granddad said. He then turned to Jake and picked him up.

'You will have to remain on the ship boy, and guard it against attack while we are gone.' Jake barked his approval.

Granddad called to the remaining three Vikings from the paintings, Arto, the Elders and knights. They all gathered round and went over their plan one more time.

Chapter 14

Graff shouted orders, readying his hideous hordes to defend the ship and stop it being boarded by Jacob and his small army. Trolls and goblins were tough to control, and they jumped around excitedly as the battle drew near. The Master watched on with her sisters by her side. Tolldruck prowled the deck, his knee fixed by some Master magic.

The Shadow King directed his walkers, hiding them all over the ship. When they were all in place, his swirling darkness could be seen moving in and out the sails. The Longship was only about one hundred metres away now, and they could see the shapes of the Vikings on board, although it was hard to see anything clearly in the darkness and the rain.

The Master and her sisters began chanting and the storm increased in intensity, battering the Longship mercilessly, yet still it came. With all their attention focused on the Longship they did not look to the sky as the gryphon silently flew down, dropping Granddad off behind all the commotion.

Every goblin and troll were watching the Longship, screaming with delight each time a large wave battered into it. Next came the eagle carrying the three Vikings and finally the dragons carrying Peter, George, the Elders and the knights. They flew with a graceful quietness that defied their size. The dark storm that filled the night provided the perfect cover.

When everyone was safely on-board Granddad turned to the Elders and nodded, all three took out one of their bombs, this time, filled with liquid sunshine, and got ready to throw them. Granddad gave the signal, and the bombs were thrown.

The sudden bright light contrasted the darkness, blinding the enemy army and creating utter confusion and terror as the liquid sunshine exploded amongst them, killing scores of goblins and trolls in seconds.

The Master threw up a protective bubble around her and her sisters cursing the stupidity at being fooled so easily. Tolldruck roared in pain as the liquid sunshine burned his skin. Unlike the others, it was not strong enough to kill him but burned him badly.

With all the chaos on the deck, the remaining Vikings on the Longship were able to board the ship and join the battle. Arto jumped on board with a ferocious deafening roar. Trolls and goblins screeched and screamed not knowing which way to face as the attack came from two sides.

'Look, Granddad!' Peter shouted, pointing just behind the witches. 'Charlotte and James are in those cages.'

'It is a trap, why else would they be out in the open?' Granddad questioned.

'We have to save them. We can't let them get hurt.' Peter replied, grabbing George and moving towards the cages.

'Vikings with me, knights go with the Elders and find the children.' Granddad shouted.

With that he set off after Peter, catching up with them just in time to meet a group of goblins head on. Peter and George both froze as the reality of the battle hit them. Granddad and the Vikings moved past, drawing swords and cutting down goblin after goblin effortlessly. They moved as a unit, taking down their enemies with blurring speed, seemingly untouchable. Granddad turned to Peter and shouted,

'Use the sunshine Peter and stay close.'

Peter snapped out of his frozen state and dragged George with him. He looked up to the cages and stopped, the witches had gone, and James and Charlotte were alone with no one guarding them.

'Granddad the cages, they are unguarded.'

Before Granddad could warn Peter to stop, he and George had moved across to the cages desperate to free their friends. Peter went to James, and George went to Charlotte.

'I knew you'd come for us.' Charlotte said to George, fear etched across her face.

George was about to answer when something dropped from the mast and grabbed him. Peter turned, as Charlotte screamed, just in time to be lifted off the ground by a swirling dark cloud. The Shadow King had them both. It had been so easy. Their plan had worked perfectly.

'I knew you would come too.' He said mocking Charlotte. He held the boy's upside down with ease and left them dangling for Granddad to see.

The Master reappeared, smiling as her eyes met Granddads.

'It appears your grandson was not ready for battle just yet Jacob, or should I call you Granddad as well?'

'Call off your Vikings or the boys will know the pain of the darkness.' She said, nodding to the Shadow King, who tightened his grip on the boys' legs making them scream.

Granddad looked around desperately for help, for something to turn the situation around.

'Who are you looking for Jacob? Maybe your knights can save you?' the Master asked as Tolldruck appeared with the two lifeless bodies, throwing them to the floor.

'Perhaps the Elders will come to your rescue?' she said beginning to enjoy herself. The Elders appeared, bound together, being carried by the other sisters.

'It seems you underestimated us and the foolishness of boys.'

Peter tried to concentrate, dangling upside down with the blood rushing to his head. He reached into his pocket and felt the water pistol still there. Slowly he pulled it out hoping the Shadow King was too busy watching Granddad being humiliated by the Master.

George watched Peter then remembered his pistol and looked for it in his pocket. His hands were not as sure as Peter's, and as it came out his pocket he lost his grip, and it fell to the ground. The movement caught the Shadow King's eye as he saw George trying desperately to make a grab for the falling gun. He twisted his darkness round to George.

'Trying to be a hero boy? What were you going to do, shoot me with your water pistol?' he asked, giving George a glimpse of his face.

'Maybe I'll shoot you with mine.' Peter said taking aim, and just as the Shadow King turned his darkness to Peter, the liquid sunshine sprayed out the pistol covering his face, spreading quickly over his body. He roared in pain, releasing the boys to fall towards the ground.

The Shadow King glowed brightly as the sheer amount of liquid sunshine overwhelmed him. He writhed in pain, helpless against the sunshine as it continued to spread. Arto charged through the goblins and trolls to try and catch the boys just as the gryphon and eagle swooped down catching them both perfectly.

The Shadow King gave one last scream and dropped to the floor using all his strength to fight and overcome the liquid sunshine. George picked up his water pistol and ran to where the King's darkness writhed and shimmered, glowing in places then burning with intense heat.

'Shooting you with my water pistol is exactly what I'm going to do.' George said taking aim and sending a stream of sunshine into the King, finishing him off once and for all. He glowed white for a moment then exploded into ashes.

The Master screamed with rage.

'Enough of these games, kill them all!' She pointed to Granddad and a bolt of blue shot from her left hand.

Granddad reacted quickly, diverting the bolt with his sword, sending it back at the Master, knocking her to the ground. Her sisters ran to help, giving the Vikings the chance to free the Elders. The battle raged on around them, and the deck was covered in the bodies of trolls and goblins while only a few Vikings had fallen.

Tolldruck watched as the Master dropped to the ground and he turned his attention to Granddad. Roaring he charged, the speed of the attack took Granddad by surprise, but Arto was quicker and intercepted, smashing into Tolldruck seconds before he would have crushed Granddad.

The pair began to struggle on the ground. Slowly Tolldruck gained the upper hand and threw Arto across the deck taking out goblins and trolls like bowling pins as he went. He didn't want to give the bear time to recover so charged after him. A large form landed on the deck blocking Tolldruck from getting to Arto.

One of the dragons roared shooting fire at Tolldruck forcing him back, turning several goblins to ash in the process. The second dragon landed on the other side blasting fire at Tolldruck, surrounding him. Granddad saw his chance and together with the three Vikings they charged Tolldruck. He brought his sword down taking off more of the beast's tail.

Tolldruck yelled in pain and surprise as one of the Vikings took off half an arm with a single stroke of his big axe. Another roar from Tolldruck and he thrashed out, catching a Viking, sending him flying like a leaf in the wind. One of the dragons flew up in the air then swooped, taking Tolldruck in its massive claws, lifting his injured body off the ship and dropping him into the sea. The dragons turned their attention to the deck again, blasting more fire, killing tens of goblins trying to run for cover.

Graff was terrified. This was not his kind of fight. Everything was going so badly. The Shadow King was dead, Tolldruck had been thrown overboard, and even the Master was injured or worse. The Vikings were too strong as they had been in the caves, even the young boys had weapons powerful enough to kill the Shadow King. He ran left and right avoiding the main areas of fighting, finally managing to roll towards the hatch and get off the deck.

The Elders, protected by the knights, advanced towards the three witches. The Master lay motionless; her sisters were preoccupied trying to wake her and did not notice the Elders approach. They took out the bottles of liquid sunshine and poured them over the head of the nearest sister while the knights attacked the other.

The witch screamed as smoke rose from her burning skin. Somehow, she found the strength to stand and shot a bright red bolt from her hand which caught Elder Andersen squarely in the chest throwing him backwards. He landed heavily on the deck unmoving. The witch turned to the other Elders cackling, with red and blue sparks dancing at her fingertips.

The sight of her was grotesque as she continued to burn; her hair fell out as she stumbled towards them. She opened her mouth to speak, and her jaw fell off. A momentary look of surprise crossed her face before the sparks stopped dancing at her fingertips and she fell forwards onto the deck.

At the same time, the knights attacked the second sister, who sensed them at the last second and with grace and speed threw herself into a backwards somersault landing out of reach of their swords. She motioned with her hand, and one of the knights was thrown twenty feet. The other charged but was met with a green bolt which dropped him on the spot. She saw her sister struggling, clearly in trouble, and was about to fly over to help her when she was grabbed from behind by powerful arms.

She could not break the iron grip no matter how she struggled. Breathing was becoming difficult as she gasped for air, howling in pain. Arto didn't let go until the witch had stopped struggling, only then did he let her drop to the ground. Elder Thomson came over and emptied the last of his liquid sunshine on to her. She sizzled and popped, giving off a greenish brown smoke.

'Now for the Master.' said Arto, striding to where she had been lying just seconds ago. The Master was gone; she was nowhere to be found.

'Find the Master, search below the decks.' Arto bellowed.

Granddad and the boys fought side by side, sword and liquid sunshine dropping many goblins and trolls. The battle was won, and soon the enemy were jumping overboard taking their chances with the sea rather than stand and fight.

Finally, Granddad sheathed his sword and took in the scene. The deck of the giant ship was covered in countless bodies of trolls and goblins. A few Vikings and knights had been killed which saddened him, but his main thoughts were for the children. He saw Elders Thomson and Sanderson leaning over the lifeless body of Elder Andersen.

Tears welled in his eyes, but there was work still to be done before they could call this day a victory and ensure no one had died in vain. He gathered his three Viking brothers and together with Arto, Peter and George they freed Charlotte and James. They sent them back to the Longship with a Viking escort before going below deck to find the rest of the children.

They could hear the cries of the terrified children somewhere below them.

'I smell Shadow Walkers, be careful.' Arto said.

The boys pointed their water pistols, ready to shoot any Walkers that crossed their paths.

'Be careful with those, remember we burn just as easily as they do.' Granddad said, drawing his sword once again after Arto's warning.

They arrived in the narrow corridor of cages where the children were being held. The Vikings and Granddad broke lock after lock with their weapons while Arto ripped bars apart using his brute strength. Eventually, all the children were free, and Granddad was trying to calm them down so he could tell them where to go to get out of the ship. He pointed to the door at the end of the corridor and stopped. A mass of black shadows guarded the entrance.

'Peter, George, stay with the children and if any Shadow Walkers get past us, you must stop them.'

The boys nodded, staying with the children as Granddad led the Vikings and Arto in an attack against the Walkers. Their resistance was futile and within a few minutes, all the Walkers were dead. Granddad signalled for the boys to bring the children as they made for the deck and back to the Longship. Once the group were gone Graff came out of his hiding place and breathed a sigh of relief. They had not won the battle, but he was alive, and that was the most important thing.

Chapter 15

The children were led on to the Longship, helped every step of the way by Vikings, and greeted by Jake who still didn't want to miss a chance to lick a face. Each child was cheered as their feet touched the Longship for the first time.

Peter and George took their turn, and Jake bounded over to Peter who had no choice but to pick him up. Charlotte ran up to George giving him a huge hug and kiss on the cheek, causing him to blush so strongly that even the night could not hide it.

Granddad and Arto were last to climb on board and just as they had joined Peter and George the gryphon returned shrieking and squawking at Granddad.

'Look over there, the Portal to the witches' world.'

Everyone on board turned and watched as the portal came into view. A large almost impossible circle appeared to be sitting on the sea. Inside there were glimpses of a strange red and green ocean and a purple sky.

The huge witches' ship moved closer and closer before finally, in a flash of brilliant light, it disappeared through the portal. The portal closed and instantly the rain stopped, the wind died down, and sea became calm.

'What happens now?' Peter asked, looking at Granddad.

'Now we go home and return all these children to their parents.'

'How will you explain the witches and the Shadow Walkers and all the things that have happened?' asked George.

'The Elders can take care of that; their magic doesn't only kill evil creatures it can be used to make people forget.'

'There are so many people, though, so much has happened, how can they do it?' James asked.

'We can freeze time for those left behind in the cove, and we can erase the memory of their children being taken from them. The children themselves will have their memories changed; there is no need for them to remember this horrible ordeal.' Elder Thomson said.

'The spell does not last long. If we had not made it in time to stop the witches taking the children to their world there would have been chaos when we returned to the Cove.' he continued.

'What about the Master, where did she go and Tolldruck, was he killed?' Peter asked.

'I don't know the answer to either of those questions, but we must assume they are alive and for that reason, we must assume they will return.' Granddad said.

With this chilling thought in all their minds, the group fell silent and became lost in their thoughts as the Longship headed for home.

When they arrived in the underground harbour, the children were led away by the Elders to be taken home and to have their memories of this night removed.

'I won't remember any of this in the morning, will I?' Charlotte asked Granddad.

'No, you will have no memory of it, and neither will your parents.' he replied.

She turned to George and Peter and hugged them both.

'Thank you for saving us, thank you for bringing us home.' She held George's hand for a minute then was led away with James.

As they walked through the mansion taking in all the damage that had been caused by the fights and by Tolldruck, the boys wondered how they could hide such a mess when daylight came.

'Magical things can happen while we sleep.' Granddad said with a wink.

Peter and George hugged Arto and shook hands with the three Vikings before going into the games room and collapsing on two large bean bags. Within seconds both exhausted boys were fast asleep.

'They fought well Jacob, he will need more training and he will need to realise his full potential, but he will make an excellent warrior, a fine guardian.' Arto said as they watched the boys sleeping.

'Come, it is time we all rested.' Granddad replied.

The boys woke to daylight and the sounds of Granddad busy in the kitchen. Confused, they looked at each other before scrambling to their feet and running out into the hall. All the damage from the previous night was gone. The dragon was back on the rug in the hall. They ran into the study to find Arto was in his rug.

'What's going on?' Peter said, looking at George.

'I'm not sure, let's find your Granddad.'

They found him in the kitchen preparing breakfast as if the previous night had not happened.

'Granddad, what happened? Where's all the mess, and the damage?'

'I told you last night, magical things can happen while we sleep.' Granddad said. 'The guardians are no longer needed in this world, all who survived have returned to their places where they will wait until they are needed again.'

'What do we do for the rest of the holiday, do we go home? I am so confused.'

'You and I have much to discuss, and you have much to learn. Something tells me the Master will not wait one hundred years to return this time. Her sisters died, and she will be looking for revenge.' Granddad said.

'Oh no, mum is going to be calling me this morning, what do I tell her?'

'You tell her it has been quite an adventure so far.' Granddad said with a smile.

Epilogue

Deep below the mansion, in the darkest coldest cave, the injured beast crawled out of the water and rested. He was exhausted and in pain, but he would survive.

Movement caught his eye, but he was too weary to move or defend himself. The Master appeared by his side placing her hand on Tolldruck's head.

'Patience my friend, we will heal you and then we will have our revenge. I have summoned someone very special. We will not be so easily defeated next time.'

Tolldruck stretched his hideous mouth into a weary smile. He knew who the Master spoke of; the only living thing he feared.

The Shifter was coming, and with him would come victory.

Thank you for reading book 1 in the series. I would love you to leave a review and share your experience with other readers. I appreciate, and read, every review that's written for my books. Click the link for your Amazon area to leave a review.

Amazon US review

Amazon UK review

Amazon Canada review

Author's notes

The Viking's Apprentice began life entitled 'Campbell's Cove'. As the story developed it became obvious this working title would need to change to give readers a better idea of what was in store in the book.

The town of Campbell's Cove is fictional but is based on a real town in Argyll in Scotland. That town is Furnace which is where Kathleen is from. The street layout is the same and I have used the location of the quarry in Furnace to place the row of mansions and beneath them the caves. Anyone who has been to that area of Scotland and driven through the hills and amazing scenery will understand why it has been such an inspiration to me.

The story of witches using eggshells to cross water was first told to me by Kathleen. It was the reason she was told to bash in your eggs shells once you had finished your boiled egg and soldiers. Witches couldn't use the shells to cross water if they were smashed. This little tale provided the inspiration for the use of the eggs in my story although I did expand and change it. I am sure Kathleen will forgive me for that!

I have taken certain liberties with the use of the Karvi Longship and its' size in my story. Due to this it should not be taken as an accurate representation of a real Karvi. To date no one has ever found an intact Longship sail so Granddad's may be the only one in existence.

Jake, the Jack Russell, in my story is basically my own Jack Russell, Megan. Anyone who owns a Jack Russell will probably see a lot of their own dog in Jake. I made Jake male so that my other dog, Ted a chocolate lab, would not feel left out!

The cover picture will no doubt attract some interest among keen historians as Vikings did not have horns in their helmets. However, ask any child to draw a Viking and the horned helmet will take pride of place. For this reason, it was decided between myself and my brother to use the horns. There is no mention of horned helmets at all in the book apart from the cover art.

The artist for this book is my very talented brother, Paul McLeod. Watching him work on the cover and getting to see his ideas and watch him pull it all together really makes you appreciate the talent and hard work that goes into it. His eye for detail is outstanding, and the finished work speaks for itself.

Kathleen has helped me throughout this book and her support and encouragement played a large part in getting it into print.

To the people who edited this book, Audra and Karen, I appreciate your work and your honesty and not least of all your patience.

About the author

Kevin McLeod lives in Hamilton, Scotland with his two daughters, Rachael and Elena. The Viking's Apprentice marks the end of a two-year journey to write a book that would fuel the imaginations of children and young adults. Kevin currently fits his writing in around his day job in Motherwell and his busy family life. As well as writing Kevin enjoys spending time with his family, walking their dogs and catching up with friends whenever the chance arises.

The Viking's Apprentice is the first book in a series, and book two entitled The Master's Revenge is available now. Read the prologue on the next page.

The Master's Revenge

Prologue

'Spirit of the Sea, this is the coast guard. Do you copy? Over.'

'I repeat. Spirit of the Sea, this is the coast guard. Do you copy? Over.'

'Coast guard this is the Captain of the Spirit of the Sea. I copy. Over.'

'Be advised we have a localized storm in your area. The storm is moving towards your vessel at a vast rate of knots. Over.'

'What kind of storm? Over'

'It looks like a twister, and it's moving fast. Be advised to take all required precautions and keep this channel open. Over.'

'Thanks for the warning. I'll leave the channel open. Over and out.'

'What was that, Bob?'

'It was the coast guard. They said there's a storm heading our way.' He paused, his hand on the ladder before continuing. 'I am going up to have a look.'

Bob Casey, the captain of the Spirit of the Sea, went above deck leaving his game of cards behind. He cursed the coast guard under his breath. He was winning the game for the first time in months. The sea seemed quiet and calm, the sound of the waves breaking off one another was all he could hear. Bob looked all around and finally he saw it, moving silently with great speed, what looked like a water twister closed in on the boat fast.

'Bob, what are you doing up h... .' Craig Miller stopped in mid-sentence when he saw the expression on Bob's face. He turned to look where Bob was staring and froze. A huge twister sped towards them. Panic erupted on board as the other two players in the card game came on deck.

The twister hit fast, lifting the Spirit of the Sea out of the water then throwing it back without breaking course. Bob held on to the mast for dear life. He raised his head against the wind and water and screamed as a hideous monstrous face appeared in the twister for just a second.

The Spirit of the Sea began to sink as those on board scrambled on to the inflatable dinghy that served as a lifeboat.

'What did you see Bob? Bob what was it?' Craig asked, grabbing hold of Bob's arm.

'I, I, I don't know, something, I saw something,' Bob said slipping down into the dinghy as Craig fired off a flare.

Continue the adventure with book #2 to find out what new evil the boys must face in:

The Vikings Apprentice II
The Master's Revenge

Contact details

www.kevinmcleodauthor.com

kevinmcleodauthor@gmail.com

https://twitter.com/bannon1975

www.facebook.com/thevikingsapprentice

https://www.instagram.com/kevinmcleodauthor

Goodreads

Printed in Great Britain
by Amazon